He dragged the stic e
*federale* post that c e
machine guns on the e
of the place; pointing

'You just persuad
ain't no way anyone c

'That's it,' said Onslow. 'That's what the guards think. They think no one can attack them.'

'They're right,' said McCloud. 'No one can.'

'No,' said Onslow. 'They're wrong. We can. Not an army, but us. Going in quiet, so they don't expect us. Not a prison break; just four men going in to take one out.'

'Yeah.' Strong was the first to speak. 'I see it, just. It wouldn't be easy, but it could be done.'

'Don't see why not,' said Jamie Durham. 'I'm willing to try.'

'You're all crazy,' said McCloud. 'We'll all get killed. It's not possible.'

'Villa's paying one thousand dollars a man,' said Onslow. 'In advance.'

'Shit!' McCloud shook his head. 'You know how to leave the best to last, don't you?'

□

THE GRINGOS – four outlawed Americans on the wrong side of the border. Fighting was all they had learned from life, money was all they wanted from it and death was all they expected.

Also by J. D. Sandon in THE GRINGOS series

*Guns Across the River*
*Cannons in the Rain*
*Fire in the Wind*
*Border Affair*
*Easy Money*
*Mazatlan*

*J. D. Sandon*

# One Too Many Mornings

A MAYFLOWER BOOK

**GRANADA**

London Toronto Sydney New York

Published by Granada Publishing Limited in 1981

ISBN 0 583 13245 6

A Granada Paperback Original


Granada Publishing Limited
Frogmore, St Albans, Herts AL2 2NF
and
3 Upper James Street, London W1R 4BP
866 United Nations Plaza, New York, NY 10017, USA
117 York Street, Sydney, NSW 2000, Australia
100 Skyway Avenue, Rexdale, Ontario, M9W 3A6, Canada
PO Box 84165, Greenside, 2034 Johannesburg, South Africa
61 Beach Road, Auckland, New Zealand

Printed and bound in Great Britain by
Cox and Wyman Ltd, Reading

Set in Plantin

'Shoot all the brave horses
And how will we ride?'
*John Stewart*

'The silent night is shattered
by the sounds inside my mind.
I'm one too many mornings and a thousand miles behind.'
*Bob Dylan*

For a man who knows his malt from his grain:
Andy McKillop

# AUTHOR'S NOTE

Most readers will be familiar with the Mexican terms used here – *hacienda, amigo, coronel,* etc. – but for a greater understanding of the military picture some explanation is worthwhile.

During the Revolution the Government maintained a standing army, which was backed up with a para-military police force, divided as follows...

The *Federales* represented the main instrument of government control (much like the *Guardia Civil* of Franco's Spain) and were based chiefly in, and around, the larger towns.

The *Rurales* controlled the hinterlands; a kind of country police force.

The *Colorados* were elite units within the *Federale* system, identified by the red band worn around the kepi; and often by their brutality.

The term *gringo* comes from the marching song adopted by American mercenaries fighting with Juarez in an earlier revolt: they sang *Green Grow The Rushes, Oh,* which their comrades-in-arms found difficult to pronounce, and so shortened the opening words to...*gringo.*

J. D. Sandon
1980.

# *Foreword*

THE Mexican Revolution began in 1910, when Francisco Madero wrested power from the tyrannical Diaz. In a little over two years, one of Madero's own generals – Victoriano Huerta – rebelled against the mild-mannered, aristocratic President and seized power for himself.

Huerta was a drunkard, a drug addict, and a brutal dictator. He clamped an iron fist on the war-torn country: so fiercely that opposition sprang up from unexpected quarters. South of Mexico City, in the 'sugar bowl' of Morelos province, a *peon* leader called Emiliano Zapata was still fighting for his vision of equality: a land where all had the right to control their destinies. To the north, in Sonora and Chihuahua, a bandit called Pancho Villa became a revolutionary. And then, in Coahuila, the Governor – Venustiano Carranza – turned against Huerta, establishing an alternative seat of government in Nogales.

Carranza raised an *army* – rather than the guerrilla forces led by Villa and Zapata – and gave command to Pablo Gonzalez and Alvaro Obregon, who formed an uneasy alliance with Villa.

The entire picture was confused, clouded by the disparate objectives of the protagonists, and their vastly different backgrounds. Zapata sought agrarian reform: his visionary policy of *Tierra y Libertad*; Villa sought wealth and power; Carranza sought to bring order without, too much, upsetting the status quo. The Revolutionary opposition was, at best, a flimsy structure of mistrust and divided aims, but the unlikely allies pressed Huerta hard. Zapata continued his advance from the south – slowly, for where he conquered he left men to till the land. Villa concentrated on a direct push from the north, using the railway system to transport his rag-tag army of bandits and camp followers. Obregon pushed down the Pacific coast to strike the capitol from the west. And all were in a hurry: anxious to reach Mexico City first; afraid to see power wrested by an ally.

And across the border, America watched with the keen eyes of self-interest. A great deal of American money was invested in the cheap labour and rich mineral resources of Mexico. The arms embargo lasting through most of 1913 and 1914 was lifted, but the bulk of the munitions sold legally to the rebels went to Carranza: the United States had little time for bandits such as Villa.

But Pancho Villa had other sources of supply. In any war there are men willing to trade their skills for a price – or a dream. And even some who agree with Zapata's words:

'It is better to die on your feet than to live on your knees.'

J. D. Sandon
1980.

# *Chapter One*

The captain commanding the squad of *Colorados* swung down from his horse with the natural grace of a born rider. He passed the reins to a trooper and lifted the dust goggles from his handsome features, stretching the elastic so that the goggles settled back against the peak of his cap, across the scarlet band with the insignia of his rank at the centre. He looked up at the pale, full moon as he eased the grey gloves from his hands, then began to slap gently at his uniform. The sound was lost under the buzzing of the cicadas, and the dust drifted softly away in the moonlight.

It was a small town, and consequently quiet at midnight. A good, sleepy place for a man to hide; not touched by the war.

The *Colorado* captain scanned the outlines of the buildings, letting his eyes confirm the information he had received back at headquarters in León. A population of around eight hundred, mostly farmers and agents handling the farmers' produce. Beyond the moonwashed bulks of the houses there would be a central plaza. It would have a fountain at the centre – probably dry. From where he stood there would be a cantina to the right and a church to the left. There would be a few stores, selling farm implements and seed. Directly across the plaza, north of the church, there would be a *Rurale* post. It would be empty.

The man in León had assured him of that.

'You're losing this war,' he had said in excellent Spanish. 'You're almost surrounded. If it goes on like this, you'll be cut off. Literally.'

The *Colorado* captain had stared at the man, wondering

why his *coronel* should allow a *yanqui* to speak that way. But *Coronel* Garcia had motioned for him to stay silent and listen.

'Valdaña's a rebel town now,' the American had continued. 'They believe Villa's close enough to take them over. They could be right.'

His voice was cold and dry, like a whisper of wind in the night. It matched his appearance: short, sandy hair, almost white, matching his suit; dark glasses so black his eyes were invisible above the thin nose and mean lips. It was difficult to tell his age, but his air of command was such that the young officer assumed him senior. Certainly important: why else would Garcia allow him to dictate policy?

'There's a revolutionary agent there.' The cold voice cut through the officer's bemusement. 'His name is Juan Oveda. He's stirred them up enough that they think they'll make a better deal with Villa than with us. I want him.'

'*We* want him.' Garcia spoke for the first time since making the introductions. 'It is in both our interests, *señor* Bender.'

'Yeah.' For a moment Hiram Bender's hidden eyes swivelled towards the colonel. '*We* want him. Alive.'

The impenetrable stare came back to fasten on the captain's face. Without thinking, the younger man stiffened his back, trying to look commanding.

'Since he got there,' continued Bender, 'food production's slowed right down. What's worse is the *Rurales* pulled out. Two got shot, and when the commander threatened to punish the town if they didn't hand over the killers, the whole lot told him he'd get killed if he didn't leave.'

The officer gasped, looking to his colonel for permission to speak. Garcia had nodded and said, 'Go ahead, Montes.'

And Raul Montes had voiced his full opinion of what should be done to a community that betrayed the government so foully, and how he would enjoy commanding the disciplinary force.

And Bender had shaken his narrow head and said, 'No. That's the worst thing we could do. Listen.'

He had paused long enough to sip water, wiping his mouth afterwards with a silk handkerchief. Then said:

'If we raize the place we just make enemies. We empty the farms and hand them over to Villa while we still need their food. What we have to do is scare them. Show them they can't fight us, not without getting into real trouble. It has to be done carefully.'

And Montes had listened while the American explained how he wanted the revolutionary, Juan Oveda, taken from Valdaña to face trial in León. So that he could be found guilty and sentenced to a prison term. Quietly; at least so far as Oveda was concerned: anyone with him could be killed, but Oveda himself had to be brought back to León for trial.

'Why?' Montes had asked. 'Why not kill him there? Or hold a public execution here?'

Bender had shaken his head some more. Like a teacher addressing a slow child.

'Your government's in a difficult situation,' he had said; slowly, choosing his words with care. 'There's people in America think the embargo should be set again. That we should support Huerta. But with the north gone over to Villa and Carranza there's no one ready to stick his neck out for your side. Wilson's backing the winners; as he sees them; and Congress agrees. What support you got from Germany is slowing down, because they're gearing up for a war of their own. So you – *we* – have to play it real careful. Oveda's got contacts in the States: he knows people there; written articles for newspapers. Kill him outright, and there'll be a campaign by the liberals against Huerta.'

He smiled. It was like watching a snake's fangs bared.

'No. We take him quietly. Bring him back here and put him in prison. That way, no one can accuse us of brutality. Then if Huerta wins, we can shoot him. If not, he'll most likely rot there.'

'You understand?' Garcia had asked. 'You know what you must do?'

Raul Montes had nodded. '*Si, coronel.*'

'Good.' Garcia had smiled. 'Excellent. Handle it well and there could be a promotion.'

Montes tugged his gloves back over his hands and lifted his pistol from the button-down holster. It was a Luger, the 9mm Parabellum model of 1908, its metal parts shining dull under the moon, its familiar contours snugging against his hand like an old friend.

He worked the toggle to spring a load into the chamber, glancing back to where his lieutenant was grouping the men. He smiled as the smooth action of the pistol slotted the cartridge into place, and waited for Hernandez to join him.

The *teniente* had left two men with the horses, grouped inside an olive grove that hid them from sight of the town. The remainder – eighteen, counting Montes and Hernandez – clustered about the wall surrounding the grove. They carried rifles, Mannlichers, with only the two officers wearing pistols.

'The place is down there.' Montes pointed across a dirt street that opened onto another dirt street. 'The house is hidden behind a wall, but it has a door opening onto the street. Make no noise.'

'*Claro,*' said Hernandez. 'We are ready.'

'Good.' Montes checked the safety catch of his Luger and led the way into Valdaña.

The town was very quiet. Perhaps too much so. Or perhaps that was just his nervous anticipation. At least, nothing happened as they paced fast down the alley and swung into the wider avenue leading to the plaza. The avenue containing the house where Juan Oveda was hiding. The moon was now at its zenith, and the cloud cover that had hidden their approach was blown away by a westerly wind, leaving the great orb shining clear over the tiled rooftops and adobe-walled streets.

Somewhere across the town a dog howled, the cry cutting short as a voice grumbled a protest. The *Colorados* flattened against the whitewashed walls until the sound ceased, then moved forwards again, trying to keep their nailed boots clear of the odd stone that jutted from the packed dirt of the avenue.

Montes had memorized the map Bender had shown him, so when he reached Oveda's house he knew exactly where he was, and motioned with his left hand for a halt.

The house was set three back from the plaza, a wide, low, two-storey construction with dark blue tiles covering the roof and a balcony surrounding three walls. The fourth wall faced onto a street that ran parallel to the plaza, with a huge, metal-studded door set between two wide windows that were covered with the same kind of basketwork grille that spanned those on the upper level. A wall ran around the house to separate it from the side alley and the buildings beyond. There was a small wooden gate in the wall, giving access to the courtyard. The windows showing along the balcony were dark, but at the front a single light glowed.

Montes whispered his men into position: three at the front, flattened into the shadows of the facing wall; three in the narrow alley on the far side; and three behind the building. Three more went into the courtyard, lining against the interior wall where their boots trampled down the flowers growing in the borders. Montes, Hernandez, and a sergeant called Varez, approached the house.

At the rear there was a smaller door, a wooden facing that appeared to open into a kitchen. It was locked.

Montes hammered on the woodwork with the butt of his Luger.

There was a long pause, and then a light showed, fluttering towards the windows. It got closer and faded, then bolts creaked and a voice that was sleepy with age grumbled an enquiry through the narrow crack of the partially-opened door. Montes saw a lined face dimly illuminated by the lantern in the old man's hand, rheumy eyes that were further gummed by slumber. He slammed his shoulder against the wood, springing the door inwards so that it struck the old man and sent him stumbling back. Montes went through fast, with Hernandez and the sergeant close on his heels.

The old man was rubbing at his cheek where the edge of the door had bruised him, the lantern swaying wildly in his gnarled hand. He looked frightened and angry at the same time; ridiculous, too, in a flowing night-shirt that was too big for his scrawny body. When he saw the pistol Montes was holding his eyes got wide. Then crossed as the *Colorado* lifted the muzzle to touch the bridge of his nose.

'If you make one sound,' whispered Montes, 'I shall kill you. Give me the lantern.'

Nodding vigorously, as though trying to scratch his nose on the Luger, the old man passed the lantern over.

Montes passed it to Hernandez and nodded to the sergeant, who stepped behind the old man with his rifle held across his chest. He brought the Mannlicher up and round in a short, vicious arc that crashed the stock against the old man's neck just below the right ear. The rheumy eyes snapped closed, and the scrawny body jerked rigid then seemed to fold in on itself. Montes caught him as he fell, lowering him to the red-tiled floor.

They were in a kitchen, the air still redolent of cooking, a fire glowing dim behind the gate of the stove. There was a door facing them. Montes opened it. Beyond was a large, sparsely furnished room, the centre of the tiled floor occupied by an ancient wooden table with a bowl of oranges in the middle. The walls were of rough-plastered adobe, partially covered with brightly woven Indian blankets. Off to the right an open door suggested the old man's sleeping quarters, and a croaking voice suggested that he might have a wife. Montes pointed at the sergeant, then at the door. The man nodded and moved silently through. There was a gasp that began to turn into a scream, but never got beyond the first hoarse inhalation of breath. Instead, it ended abruptly with the soggy sound of a blow sinking into soft flesh.

The sergeant came back into the room, his dark face impassive as he lifted one finger and then made a chopping motion. Montes smiled and pointed at the stairs leading off from the left. Hernandez raised the lantern, casting its glow on polished wood that led up to an interior balcony. Montes understood the warning, and pressed a finger to his lips.

He grasped the stair rail, setting a foot cautiously on the first step, as far from the centre as he could manage. Then – holding close to the side, where the boards were less likely to creak – he began to sidle upwards. Hernandez and the sergeant followed with the same exaggerated caution.

There were four doors opening off the balcony, all closed and dark as coffin lids. Montes wondered which one Oveda used, then decided the only way to find out was to check them all. He eased towards the closest, motioning for Hernandez to douse the light. The *teniente* shut down the wick and pinched out the flame, then set the lantern carefully on the boards. He stepped to the right side of the door as the sergeant positioned himself at the centre of the balcony and Montes set his left hand on the doorknob.

It turned smoothly, and the door swung back on oiled hinges, soundless. Moonlight filtered through slatted shutters, outlining a bed that held the shape of a body. The captain crossed the room, grateful for the woven rugs covering the floor. He saw a spread of long, dark hair, blue-black in the moonlight that fell in bars across the rumpled sheet; a breast, partially exposed where the nightdress had ruckled and slipped down; a wide, full-lipped mouth, slightly parted in sleep. For an instant he felt a flood of lust: it would be so easy to take her, right now. But no: his mission was to capture Juan Oveda, and if the revolutionary got warning, then the whole filthy town could turn out against the *Colorados*.

But still, perhaps later . . .

He settled one gloved hand over the sleeping woman's mouth, raising the Luger to point at her face as she woke.

His eyes were huge, the whites emphasizing the intensity of her terrified stare as she tried to scream and felt her voice cut off by the clamping hand.

Hernandez dropped across the bed, pinning her legs before she even had a chance to kick.

'I don't want to kill you,' said Montes, very softly. 'But I will if I must.' He tapped her gently with the pistol. 'If you tell me where Oveda is, I might let you go. If you try to warn him, I shall have to kill you.'

Slowly, warily, he took his hand from her mouth.

'You've come to kill him,' she said, her voice husky with sleep and fear. 'For what he's done.'

'No.' Montes angled the Luger at her clean, white teeth. 'I've come to arrest him. That's all. You have my word on that.'

'Your word?' She made it an insult. 'How much is that worth?'

'How much is a bullet worth?' said Montes. 'Or a day with my men? Tell me!'

'*Jesus Cristo!*' The words came softly through a miasma of fear. '*Madre de Dios!*'

Montes cut the babble by the simple expedient of thrusting the barrel of the Luger between her teeth, shoving it far enough in that the root of the tongue was flattened, the foresight digging into her throat.

'I don't want to kill him,' he said. 'My orders are to arrest him; nothing more. I don't want to kill anyone, but if you don't help me – well . . . '

He left the sentence unfinished as he eased the German pistol from the woman's mouth.

Her face was pale now, almost green in the shadowed clarity of the moon, and her teeth chattered as the cold metal of the pistol withdrew. Her eyes fixed with stark intensity on the captain's face. Then closed as some kind of spasm worked over her features and she said – very softly, very quietly – 'In the next room. He often sleeps there.'

'The other rooms?' asked Montes, still holding the gun pointed at her face. 'Are there other people here?'

'No.' She shook her head. 'God forgive me! There's no one else.'

'Montes smiled and slid an arm under her shoulders, easing her to a sitting position. 'Thank you,' he said; formally. 'Please come with us.'

Hernandez lifted clear of the bed and went over to the door. Montes watched the woman rise, tug on a gown of plain white cotton, and took her by the elbow. As though escorting her to some reception. She let him guide her, her eyes wide and her face blank. The *Colorado* kept the Luger pressed against her temple.

Juan Oveda was stretched on a narrow couch with a book open on his stomach. One hand touched the floor, close by a mug of cold coffee. Beside the mug, partly hidden under the bed, was a Colt's Thunderer in .41 calibre.

Juan Oveda didn't like guns. They frightened him the same way most tools frightened him: he wasn't very good with tools. What he liked was ideas; words, and the way they affected people. That he understood; knew how to use them the way a carpenter knows how to use an adze to shape a piece of wood the way he wants it, or a gunfighter knows how to use a weapon to maximum effect. Oveda wouldn't even have been in Valdaña if Carranza hadn't asked – which was much the same as ordering – him to rouse the *peons* to the revolutionary cause.

He was fifty years old, and most of his life had been spent writing about the wrongs perpetrated on, and in, Mexico. He had been one of the first to support Madero, convincing American businessmen that it was worth lending money to the next President of Mexico; writing articles about the struggle, introducing Francisco to all the influential people he knew. And then Francisco handed control of the Army to Huerta. And died. And Huerta had established a regime of terror that equalled anything Diaz had set up, so Oveda had quit Mexico City and gone back to Coahuila. Crossed the border to spend more time in the United States trying to explain why a bandit like Pancho Villa was necessary to the revolutionary cause. And then returned to his homeland when Carranza came out in the open against Huerta.

That had seemed like the first light of hope dawning: a civilized man taking command of the revolution. Taking it away from the bandits like Villa, or the insane dreamers like Zapata. There was a balance, after all. Mexico was a polyglot country of pure Spaniards and *mestizos* and *peons*. It was crazy to think that a peasant sugar farmer like Zapata should dictate policy: Give the land back to the people? They wouldn't know what to do with it. And Villa? A bandit! All he wanted was loot and some safe place to drink out his old age. No! Carranza was the answer. He was educated. A *hacendado* who understood the needs of the people, which were to be governed by the natural elite whilst receiving a decent wage for a good day's work.

So Juan Oveda had offered his services to Venustiano Carranza and found himself shipped off to Valdaña. It was needful, Venustiano had said, so as to arouse the people. After all, Villa was approaching fast, and if he took control the entire province might go over to the bandit's side. Better, then, to establish a firm platform of reform, with a Carranzista in control. And yes, throw out the Huerta forces by all means; throw out the *rurales*. But let the people know that it was Carranza who organized it.

Captain Raul Montes saw a short, slightly fat man with a balding head and a thick beard sprawled on a stained couch. The shutters were wide open, but only reflected moonlight came into the room. It was still bright enough that the captain could see the books lining the walls, and read the title of the volume spread over the man's belly. It was a cardboard bound volume entitled *Becoming Free* by someone called Jaime Laurenzino.

Montes had never heard of the man, but he picked up the book with distaste and dropped it on the floor as he kicked the Colt clear of Oveda's hand, sliding it under the bed where it banged against the wall; well out of range.

Oveda woke up and Montes jammed the Luger against his face. Behind him, *teniente* Hernandez dragged the woman's arms back and pressed a matching pistol to her face.

Montes smiled and said, 'You're coming with us. To stand trial.'

Oveda started to ask why, but the *Colorado* smashed the butt of the Luger against his jaw, cutting the skin and splintering two teeth. Oveda groaned and rolled sideways, spitting blood. Montes hit him again, then gestured for the sergeant to step forwards.

Sergeant Varez produced a length of cord from his tunic and swung two expert loops around Oveda's wrists, binding his hands together and fastening them to his waist.

Hernandez said, 'What about the woman, *capitán*?'

And Montes smiled again and said, 'Bring her along. Quietly.'

'No.' Oveda moaned through the blood in his mouth. 'For God's sake! she's my wife.'

Montes laughed and ushered the others from the room. On the balcony he paused long enough to relight the lantern, turning the wick up high so that a tall column of fire clouded smoke around the glass funnel. Then he tossed it inside the room Oveda had occupied. The lantern shattered, spreading kerosene over the boards that was ignited by the still-burning wick. Flames licked hungrily through the liquid, reaching up to take hold of the covers of the couch and the papers on the desk; take hold of the books and begin to burn the wood.

Montes laughed again and followed the others out of the house.

The *Colorados* left Valdaña in a hurry. Juan Oveda was

strapped belly-down across the saddle of a spare horse and his wife was seated in front of lieutenant Hernandez. Her hands were lashed together on the saddlehorn, and the officer steered his mount one-handed; the other fondled the woman's breasts. Behind them, a column of flame stretched up against the dark sky. It was yellow, filled with fluttering gusts of red. It went on burning until the dawn blotted it out and they made camp.

'You can't! You promised!'

'I promised I came to arrest your husband,' replied Montes. 'That was all. Nothing more.'

'No,' she said as he reached out to tear her nightdress away. 'Please God! No!'

Montes laughed and eyed her body. She was younger than her husband: firm at breast and belly, with long legs that ended in a wide thatch of pubic hair. She staggered back, seeking to cover herself with her hands.

Across the clearing her husband shouted, 'Bastards! Leave her!' And then sergeant Varez clubbed him silent and he slumped sideways from the tree to which he was bound with blood running down his cheek. Varez grinned, and scraped the butt of his Mannlicher on the grass, thinking that he would have third turn and that she was a better-looking woman than any of the whores he knew in León. He went on watching as *el capitán* hit the woman twice across the face and called for a blanket. Watched some more as it was spread over the grass and the woman's semi-conscious body rolled onto the cover. The captain took off his Sam Browne belt and dropped his pants. His buttocks were very white as they pounded up and down in the warm morning air. They reminded Varez of a trooper he had known back in Zacatecas, before the Villistas took the town. But this was better; this was the real thing. He watched *el teniente* take his turn on the woman and then passed his rifle to the nearest man as he moved forwards, his hands already fumbling at the buttons on his pants.

All eighteen *Colorados* attacked Maria Oveda, and when they were done the woman's thighs were greased with blood and sperm. Her hair was lank with sweat, and her eyes were closed and her lower lip bitten through. Her body looked wasted, ugly bruises circling her wrists and ankles, teeth marks showing on her neck and face and breasts. Mostly, though, she looked weary, drawn in on herself as if the multiple rape had somehow drained her body.

It was noon before they had finished with her and Montes said, 'Kill the bitch.'

They got her on her feet. It took three men to lift her and hold her in position as her husband moaned and screamed and cursed them. And then four more, two to each hand as they lifted her arms against the branches of the tree and hammered the bayonets in.

They pushed them through the palms, then used rifle butts to drive the blades deep into the wood. The woman came to as they were doing it, starting to scream and vomit with the pain. Varez punched her hard in the mouth, breaking teeth, and then she got quiet for a while. Until Montes came forwards with a bayonet in his hand and dug it into her belly. Then she began screaming again, and sprayed a thick spurt of urine that was mingled with blood and semen over the captain's boots. It angered him: he drove the bayonet deep into her stomach and twisted the blade, carving it round so that an enormous hole was opened in her abdomen. A circular flap of skin opened from her belly like a trap door, and a sticky spread of entrails, all yellow and blue and white and red, burst out. Montes jumped back, nostrils pinching in at the stink, then moved to the side and slashed the bayonet back and forth over the woman's face.

By the time his rage had abated, Maria Oveda was a tattered ragdoll, her handsome features lost under a curtain of gaping flesh and dripping blood. Her belly was an open hole that draped entrails in long, steaming swathes over her legs.

Flies were already clustering on the feast as Montes

dropped the blade and turned towards his horse. There was a long silence as the *Colorados* mounted up and rode away, and then the clearing got loud with the buzz of insects and the swift scuttling of scavenging animals, anxious to benefit from another profit of the war. And the *Colorados* headed back to León with Juan Oveda draped over a saddle, barely conscious; barely sane any more.

There were witnesses at the trial, just to show that it was all done in the open; above board. So as to establish the legality of Huerta's system. Three German observers watched the entire proceeding, accompanied by two Americans Bender had brought in from Vera Cruz. The judge was dressed in black, with a powdered white wig on his head. There was even a jury: made up of Army officers. Oveda had been fed for three days after a diet of beans and mouldy bread, and the *Colorados* had been careful not to bruise him where it could show.

He was still in a state of shock, so that his evidence – presented, of course, by a duly appointed lawyer who sympathized with Huerta – was incoherent. In fact, it sounded like the ramblings of a madman. Which was exactly what the 'disinterested' observers wanted to hear.

Oveda came off badly: there wasn't any other kind of outcome, but at least he wasn't sentenced to death. Instead, he was sentenced to something worse.

Outside of León, in the mountains bordering the city, Huerta had established a prison. It was a fort of a place. Thirty-foot walls of reinforced stone stood rock-solid from a sandstone base. Ridges of sun-washed rock covered three sides, affording the watch-towers a clear field of fire down the open ends while denying any kind of reasonable approach except towards the massive, metal-barred gates. There were machine guns in the towers mounted at each corner, and two more covering the entrance. *Federale* patrols scoured the surrounding hills twice a day, and when the prisoners – those lucky enough to be on a work detail rather than confined inside a stinking, sunless cell – were taken out, they were escorted by guards armed with Winchester rifles and shotguns.

Oveda heard his sentence pronounced: sixty years in Santa Granada.

It was the same as condemning him to death, but none of the observers chose to comment on that minor fact. After all, the Huerta regime had proved its humanity by granting the man his life.

Hadn't it?

# Chapter Two

The sounds inside his mind coalesced into colours, and he smiled in his sleep, his body slowly relaxing from the tight foetal ball. The bells became glittering waves of golden light, and the clatter of horses' hooves were dark blue splashes on the gold. The hiss of steam escaping from a locomotive was a thin, straight line of green; the rumble of the wheels, a wavering band of rusty ochre. The colours swirled and danced, a fresh shade introduced for each sound from outside the tent. And Jamie Durham gave himself up to them, and let them wash over him and carry him away into sleep.

He turned onto his back, fair hair rumpled and lank with sweat, the right side of his face calm, handsome. The left was hideous. From temple to jaw a puckered mass of purple scar tissue transformed his features into a weirdly grinning mask, the eye and mouth tugged out of line by the tautening effect of the wasted skin. His arms stretched loose beside him, the undersides of the forearms tracked with needle marks: ugly red indentations that followed the lines of the veins.

Jamie Durham was a morphine addict.

Still in his twenties, he had spent years pursuing a single purpose: finding enough of the drug that he could stay sane. It wasn't his fault. It was a thing imposed on him by Army doctors in an attempt to save his life after the accident. Jamie had been one of the youngest soldiers in the Army of the United States; an expert with explosives who had payed the price of his expertise: a mine he was defusing had gone off in his face. He was lucky – from one point of view – to have survived, but survival had entailed months spent in an Army hospital, where the only comfort for his agony was morphine.

He had emerged an addict. He had taken his pension and spent it all on the drug he craved, wandering around the border territories finding work wherever anyone needed a man good with explosives. Wherever anyone could bear to look at his face. Wherever he could find the narcotic on which his life now depended.

And he had met a man called Yates McCloud, who had the right contacts. And then met two other men who offered him some kind of hope.

And that was how he came to be laying on a narrow campbed in a tent in central Mexico, his drug-fuddled mind translating the sounds of Pancho Villa's trainborne army into comforting colours.

'I thought he was weaning off that stuff.' Jonas Strong's ebony features glistened in the fire glow outside the tent. 'He looked like he was getting better.'

'Hell!' Yates McCloud dragged a cleaning rod through the barrel of his Colt's Lightning. 'He ain't using so much, but he'll never get off it.'

The Southerner's voice was matter-of-fact, and he didn't bother raising his weakly handsome face in the Negro's direction. Strong went on slotting shells into the loading gate of the Remington pump-action scattergun, but his brown eyes fastened on McCloud's down-turned head and his mouth curled in contempt.

'And that don't matter to you. Does it, Yates?'

'No.' McCloud snapped the cylinder into place and checked the alignment. 'I don't reckon to plot anyone's path to hell. That's something we all choose for ourselves!'

Strong opened his mouth to say something more, then thought better of it. He didn't like McCloud, and knew that the Southerner had little affection for him. They were a team bound together by the intricate web of professionalism and nothing more. The Mexicans called them the Gringos, setting an emphasis on the word so that it somehow came out with a capital *G*, setting them apart from the other American mercenaries working with the revolutionaries. Strong himself was there because of his loyalty – his friendship – with Cade Onslow. They had served together in the Army of the United States; until Onslow's Mexican wife was killed by Huerta's men, and the major – despite their friendship, Strong still thought of Onslow as *the Major* – had quit his command to find and kill the man responsible. Strong had gone with him. Along the way they had picked up Jamie Durham, who would only agree to lend his talent with explosives if Yates McCloud got brought along, too. That had meant breaking McCloud out of jail. Since then, they had performed the same kind of service more than once: McCloud had an ugly temper that got stoked up by the liquor he was too fond of. And a penchant for beating up on women.

And yet they made a dangerously effective team. Onslow was the planner, the leader; Jamie – the Kid, they called him – was superb with explosives; McCloud was an excellent gunhand and a cunning organizer. Strong had to admit that Yates could find supplies where no one else would think of looking; even if they were too often drugs and liquor and women.

And Jonas Strong? Well – the big Negro thumbed the last shell into the cut-down shotgun and swung the leather carrying strap over his shoulder, his fingers stroking the smooth wood of the pistol grip – well, he was muscle and back-up. Maybe a kind of levening force, a mediator between Onslow and McCloud.

And they did make a good team. One way or another, they made a very fine team. Which didn't mean that Strong had to like McCloud.

Or, he reminded himself, McCloud like him.

But at least the Southerner didn't call him 'nigger' any more.

'Wonder what they're talkin' about,' he said casually. 'The Major's been in there a long time.'

McCloud settled cartridges into the Lightning and shoved the pistol snug inside the holster before replying.

'You know what Villa's like,' he said. 'Talk the arse end off a donkey for the sake of seeing it shit.'

'Not this time.' Strong lifted the pot from the fire and filled two mugs with coffee. 'This long means they're workin' something out.'

'I guess,' said McCloud, accepting the mug Strong offered him. 'I guess it means we go bare our arses again.'

Strong grinned. 'That's why the man pays us, Yates.'

'Yeah,' was all McCloud said.

Villa's advancing army was halted between Aguascalientes and Lagos, at a water halt called Revuelto. There was nothing to the place except a few deserted adobe shacks and the wooden platform where engineers could feed water from the pump into their engines. Lagos, according to the scouts was getting rapidly deserted as the threat of the advancing Villistas spooked the inhabitants. But León was another matter. Apart from Celaya, it was the last large town before Mexico City, and Villa anticipated heavy fighting there. Lagos, he thought, would fall easily. There would probably be some resistance, but nothing large enough to worry about: the worst of the fighting would occur at León. Even so, he wanted to rest his conquering army; give the horses a period of exercise after the long days on the trains. So he had halted at Revuelto.

Now the Army of the North was spread in ragged lines about the tracks. Men exercised the horses pent up too long on the cattle cars, or spent themselves with the women accompanying the horde. The late afternoon air was filled with the multiple odours of food and horses and oil, the smell of burning wood and that of unwashed bodies; of rusty metal and steam. It was loud with laughter, for the bandit army felt confident now, and before long they would see the spires of Mexico City and take their pleasures in soft beds, between clean sheets, with wine and tequila to drink from cut crystal glasses while food was brought on silver plates.

It didn't matter that few of them knew what cut crystal was, and fewer still had seen silver plates. That was how the *hacendados*, the land-owners, lived; and that was what they would take away from the oppressors.

And soon. Yes! soon. Just a little bit more fighting. A little bit more killing. And then – Mexico City!

Pancho Villa's tent was set a little bit apart from the others. It was no larger, but it had an awning spread outside, with a trestle table and several chairs lined under the canvas overhang. There were bottles of tequila and pulque on the table, and a big bowl of olives. Villa was seated in a massively-carved chair brought down from the command train, with two hawk-eyed *dorados* behind him.

He was not a particularly impressive man, not at first sight. His face was round, almost plump, with a heavy moustache decorating his upper lip. His eyes were narrow and dark; bland, except when they flashed in anger, which came as often as did his humour. He had an easy laugh that turned just as easily to a cruel smile. Indeed, he could be cruel: he had been known to line up prisoners and see how far a single bullet would penetrate the bodies. And he had been known to set a man free because he had fought bravely.

He was an enigma. A bandit from the north who had risen to become one of the greatest powers in Mexico, commanding the allegiance of thousands. Feared by Carranza and Huerta; loathed by the United States and loved by his followers. He was barely literate. His tactics were dictated by the exigencies of the moment, by a quixotic impulse and a lust for power that had nothing to do with any of the military manuals, and yet worked with devastating effect.

He was, simply, Pancho Villa. The bandit who could bring dictators to their knees.

He smiled at the man seated across the table.

The man was pushing fast towards forty, but his body was

lean as that of a man half his age. His hair was brown, combed roughly back from a wide forehead that showed pale frown lines through the deep tan. Strands of grey showed faintly in the hair, but his moustache was thick, and there was about him an air of hardness, an indefinable aura of cool authority. He wore a flat-crowned stetson, its original colour black, but now stained with dust and sweat, like his pants. His shirt, too, showed signs of wear, fraying at the cuffs and collar, with dark sweat stains under the arms and down the back. It was crossed by the thin straps of a shoulder rig, and beneath his left arm there hung a wooden holster containing a Mauser automatic pistol in 7.63mm. Around his narrow waist there was a military-style gunbelt, the holster cut away to reveal the butt of a .45 Colt's Automatic. The military issue, available only to Army officers.

His name was Cade Onslow.

'That's the craziest thing I ever heard of,' he said. 'There's no way it can be done.'

Villa reached over the table to fill Onslow's mug with tequila.

'It must be done, Cade.' He filled his own glass. 'I don't like it, but it must be done.'

'Why?' Onslow sipped the liquor and reached for the lemon and salt. 'Leave him there.'

'And give that *hacendado* a chance to say that Pancho Villa betrayed him?' Villa licked salt and pepper and lemon and then tossed the tequila down. 'So that if Obregon reaches Mexico City before me, he can say I betrayed a revolutionary?'

'What's it matter?' Onslow shrugged. 'You'd need an army to break into that place. An' the only army you got is heading for Mexico City.'

'An army,' said Villa, 'or just a few men. I think it could be done. By the right men.'

'No,' said Onslow. 'No way. Not us.'

'You could do it.' Villa's fleshy lips spread in a smile. 'You have all the qualifications. Look.'

He raised his hand and began to count points on the fingers. They were thick, almost stubby, with dirt-grained nails and callouses on the knuckles.

'You understand military thinking, and you command three men who are very good at their business. The young one – the addict – is good with explosives. The Southerner has a way of finding things, and the black man is powerful. I would give you all the ammunition and the explosives you need. Also, I think I could offer you one thousand dollars apiece. American dollars. In advance.'

'In advance?' queried Onslow. 'You're getting almighty generous. Why?'

Villa shrugged. 'I have the money and I need the man free. You know I can't afford to mount a full-scale attack. That's why I want you to do it.'

'You that worried about Carranza?' Onslow swallowed tequila. 'He got you scared?'

For a moment Villa's face got red and ugly with anger. Onslow wondered if he had gone too far. Then the features settled back into the bland smile.

'I am not afraid of Carranza,' said the bandit. 'Nor of Obregon or Gonzalez or Zapata. But I am worried. This man, Oveda, is one of Carranza's, but Carranza sent him down here to organize support that would help me. Do you understand?'

'Yeah.' Onslow nodded, seeing now that Villa was beginning to understand the intricacies of internecine politics. 'Maybe I do.'

'If I make no attempt to save the man,' continued Villa, 'then Carranza can say I failed to support the revolution. He did everything he could – even sent a man to help me – but I let him down. Left the man to die.'

'And even if you get to Mexico City first,' said Onslow, 'he could still use that against you.'

'*Si.*' Villa nodded. 'Now you understand it.'

'I still ain't saying I'll do it,' said Onslow. 'I'll have to ask the others.'

Villa nodded and reached under the table. He lifted a heavy sack onto the wood and tugged open the draw-strings.

'Four thousand dollars, Cade. I'll also give you horses and supplies. In advance.'

Onslow emptied his glass. 'I'll put it to them. When you want to know?'

'The sooner the better,' said Villa. 'There is little time to waste.'

'All right.' Onslow stood up. 'I'll come back soon as I got an answer.'

'It can wait until morning.' Villa smiled as a large-breasted *soldadera* came out of the tent with a pout on her face and most of her blouse unbuttoned. 'I have more important matters to discuss.'

'Yeah.' Onslow turned away. 'I guess you do.'

Villa's laughter followed him across the camp.

By now it was common knowledge that Onslow had sided with the Villistas because Huerta's troops had killed his wife. That was understandable; honourable; what wasn't was why he still refused the advances of the women. In the main, he could have taken his pick: he was good-looking enough, and he had a reputation that attracted them. But he hadn't been known to sleep with a woman since joining the advance; and that was something that confused and amused the Mexicans. After all, the other Gringos did. Yates McCloud spread his seed like a farmer anxious to plough fresh meadows. *El Cicatriz* – which was what they called Jamie Durham behind his back – took a girl when he could; when the drug let him. And the big black one was not averse to comfort in the night.

But Onslow? No.

Never.

He was chaste as a monk.

And just as determined to follow his own path. It was crazy.

'It's crazy,' said McCloud. 'I heard about that place. It's a goddam fort.'

'Jamie?' Onslow looked at the Kid. 'What do you think?'

Jamie Durham rubbed at his eyes, then scratched his arms. 'I can blow any wall you show me, Cade. Get me to it – I'll blow it. But you gotta get me there.'

'We can get there,' said Strong. 'Gettin' out will be the hard part. Gettin' back with Oveda.'

'Look,' said Onslow, 'here's the set-up Villa showed me.'

He swept a patch of sand clear and picked a twig from the fire. Using the burning end he scraped two lines on the ground, like an open ended vee. At the centre he drew a square, then etched a line across the widest part.

'The prison is here.' He dug the stick into the square. 'Back here.' He traced the line at the widest part again. 'There's a rail station. It's got *federales* manning machine guns on both sides of the tracks. They end there. They come up from León with all the prisoners on board. The *federales* check them off and load them on wagons to take them up to Santa Granada.'

He traced a thin line between the deep cut and the square.

'They got machine guns on the towers.'

He dug the stick deep into the four corners of the square.

'And they send out patrols each day. Into the hills.'

'The more you talk,' said Yates McCloud, 'the less I like it.'

'It ain't easy,' said Onslow, 'I can't deny you that, Yates. But I think you're overlooking something.'

'Way you put it,' grunted the Southerner, 'I could be overlooking one hell of a lotta machine guns.'

'Yeah, you're right,' said Onslow. 'But you still get the money.'

'Can't spend it if I'm dead,' said McCloud. 'I like my money in my hand. Where I can feel it.'

'Go on,' said Strong. 'You got some kinda idea, don't you?'

'I think so,' answered Onslow. 'I think it's worth trying.'

'So try it on us,' McCloud downed his third mug of pulque. 'Convince us.'

'All right,' said Onslow, 'I'll try.'

He dragged the stick back over the lines, pointing out his own doubts; pointing out the *federale* post that covered the train halt; pointing out the machine guns on the walls of the prison; pointing out the size of the place; pointing out the patrols.

'You just persuaded me, Major,' said McCloud. 'There ain't no way anyone can get in there.'

'That's it,' said Onslow. 'That's what the guards think. They think they're safe. They think no one can attack them.'

'They're right,' said McCloud. 'No one can.'

'No,' said Onslow. 'They're wrong. We can. Not an army, but us. Going in quiet, so they don't expect us. Not a prison break; just four men going in to take one out.'

'Yeah.' Strong was the first to speak. 'I see it, just. It wouldn't be easy, but it could be done.'

'Don't see why not,' said Jamie Durham. 'I'm willing to try.'

'You're all crazy,' said McCloud. 'We'll get killed. It's not possible.'

'Villa's paying one thousand dollars a man,' said Onslow. 'In advance.'

'Shit!' McCloud shook his head. 'You know how to leave the best to last, don't you?'

'All right,' Onslow looked round at them, each in turn. 'In favour?'

'I'll go along,' said Jonas Strong.

'And me,' said Jamie Durham.

'Shit!' McCloud shrugged. 'Why the hell not?'

'In that case, gentlemen.' Onslow stood up, parodying a bow. 'I'll go tell Pancho that he owes us four thousand dollars.'

He went over to the tent occupied by the revolutionary leader. It was dark now, and the two guards were sitting at the table, drinking pulque. From inside the tent there came the moaning of a woman and the hoarser grunting of a man.

'Tell me in the morning,' said Onslow. 'When he's awake. I got business to discuss with him.'

The guards nodded, and went back to their drinking.

# *Chapter Three*

After the trial they took Juan Oveda back to his cell. Now that the pretence of justice had been observed there was no further need to coddle him, so he got flung onto the filthy straw with a kick to help him on his way. It was almost a relief to go back on the diet of beans and bread, because the richer food had given him diarrhoea. And because no one bothered to clean his cell, the place was stinking. He curled his rapidly-thinning body into a ball in the cleanest corner of the lightless room and did his best to ignore the cockroaches as he sought for sleep.

In the morning he was surprised to be given a decent cup of coffee and a hunk of fresh bread. More surprised to be taken out of the cell into the yard. He blinked in the sunlight, wondering what was happening as he scratched at the sores on his body.

The trial had left him confused. Indeed, after watching Maria die he felt confused about most things. It was as though the world had suddenly slipped out of kilter, like the cogs of a windmill becoming unmeshed so that each disc spun close, but separate to, the linked wheel. He knew that *Colorados* had taken him and his wife out of Valadaña. Knew that Maria had been raped and brutally murdered. Knew that he had been beaten. Knew that he had been tried and sentenced. Knew that the Huerta regime intended him to die.

But all the events were separated in his mind. Somehow they didn't quite mesh together, so that each one was viewed as an individual incident, divorced from the others.

He was probably mad at that point. He had suffered a

massive psychological shock. He had seen his wife die; horribly. Felt the dark threat of death touch him. And found himself totally unable to fight against the events. So perhaps his mind had taken over his thoughts in protective reaction: to compart each event to separate episodes was a way of fending off the horror of what was happening to him: what would happen to him.

Whatever; he stood subdued and silent in the courtyard as *federales* sluiced him with fresh water. He even enjoyed the cold clarity of the water, feeling it wash the blood and the bugs from his body. He didn't mind being naked: his clothes, after all, were filthy with blood and vomit.

He stared stupidly at the tunic a *Colorado* tossed at his feet, watching the water soak into the cloth as he thought that it looked like the blood he had seen matting his wife's hair. It eased up slowly, working its way through the fibres of the coarse tunic the same way the semen and blood had pulsed slowly from between Maria's thighs.

Someone said, 'Put it on, bastard.'

And he reached down and covered his nakedness with the soaking linen. And then someone rammed a rifle butt into his back and he staggered forwards, following the prodding of the gun out through the gates and onto the train.

He couldn't remember the journey to the station, nor how he boarded the closed car. The first time he could remember anything at all was when he felt something hot spray over his legs and smelled the stink of urine.

It was oppressive. Suffocating; filling his nostrils with an ammonia odour that brought him upright with one hand waving before his face.

'I thought you were dead.'

He couldn't see the speaker. The car had no windows. Just a sliding door, and he was too far from the entrance to enjoy any light.

'*De nada,*' he said. 'It doesn't matter.'

'Let me help you.'

The voice got closer, and he felt a hand reach under his back to lift him up to a sitting position.

It was less comfortable than stretching on the floor, but he felt more human there. He looked around: and saw the sorry remnants of humanity, spaced like worn-out puppets around the interior of the car.

'My name is Ramon Cortez,' said the voice. 'What's yours?'

'Juan Oveda,' he said. 'Why are you here?'

'I killed three *federales.*' Through the darkness came pride. 'They tried to take my sister, so I killed them. What did you do?'

'I knew Carranza,' said Oveda. 'I tried to help Pancho Villa.'

A hand reached out of the dark to clutch his, and Cortez said, 'Then we are friends. We'll stick together.'

'If we live,' said Oveda. 'Thank you.'

'*De nada.*'

The train moved through a day and a night and a second day. Periodically it halted to take on water and fuel. When it stopped, the two cars behind the locomotive stayed closed. There was no food given to the prisoners, nor any water. The tin drum that had been supplied on the first day ran out on the second. Nine men died in the heat.

And then the train halted.

The doors slid open, and inside came a lancing band of sun's light that pierced like needle pricks against eyes that had adjusted to darkness. There was a line of *federales* outside the train, each one holding a rifle pointed at the stinking darkness of the truck. They laughed as the shambling figures came stumbling out.

'Come on,' said Cortez. 'Let's go.'

Oveda climbed to his feet, assisted by the younger man. He clutched at his pants, unpleasantly aware of the acid tang of his bowels.

He went down the steps, following the line of *federales.*

There was a wagon at the end of the line. A tall, wide-bottomed wagon with a stepladder going up to the unwelcoming cage that took the place of the canvas. There were bars of solid steel hooping over the base, with cross-cut horizontals running at foot-wide intervals around the uprights.

There were no seats.

Oveda slumped down on the floor as the door swung shut and a *federale* turned the key in the lock.

And the wagon stumbled forwards, spilling the occupants hind over butt as the mules thrust into the traces and began to turn the wheels.

Mounted *federales* rode alongside and behind, Mannlicher rifles canted against their thighs. Two men guided each wagon, one handling the reins of the six mule team while the other sat with a shotgun on his knees. The day was hot, the sun baking down off the redrock walls of the canyon so that the men inside the cages sweated and began to dehydrate. Oveda thought that he might die. Almost welcomed the event: release. But he didn't – or couldn't – and so stayed in that intermediary stage between sanity and madness, lost to the reality of what was happening to him even as he saw it going by. Like a man in a dream. A fever dream: seeing with total clarity the events whilst refusing to understand them.

They came to Santa Granada, and from under the tall stone walls the gates opened. A squad of guards came out with Lee Enfield rifles pointed at the three wagons. And the doors got opened so that the prisoners, the condemned men, could shuffle down and group on the hot sand.

The wagons were driven off into the shade.

The guards wore kepis, peaked high at the front so that their faces were shaded, with long white squares of cotton hanging down at the back to protect their necks from the heat.

The prisoners had nothing. And they were kept standing in the sun while the wagons got turned around and the mules were watered. Then the drivers and the escorting riders ate. It was noon, and the sun bled pure white heat over the central square of the prison.

Three men fainted.

The guards kicked them, and when only one managed to get back on his feet, they dragged the others away. No one saw what happened to them, but there were two short, sharp explosions.

And then a fat man came out from the building at the centre of the complex. He was little more than five feet tall, with a belly that thrust the buttons of his khaki shirt apart and strained the limits of his Sam Browne belt.

'I am *Coronel* Alcaza,' he bellowed, strutting like an overfed turkey up and down the ranks of the prisoners. 'I command Santa Granada. So! You do what I tell you. You won't enjoy it. I promise you that. But if you don't like it, then I can think of worse things. Remember that while you are here.'

Oveda said nothing.

Just stood in line; silent.

Waiting.

He didn't have to wait long: Alcaza read out lists of names, matching each one to a crime, and then announcing the sentence.

Juan Oveda, for crimes committed against the state; against the government; was sentenced to sixty years. In a cell. No privileges.

Nothing.

The cell was small and smelly.

It was underground, so there were no windows. Just four walls of solid stone with a floor and a ceiling. The ceiling dripped water faster than the walls, making the straw on the floor sodden no matter how he arranged it. The door had an opening at the centre, a small porthole that was covered on the outside by a circle of steel plate. At the base there was a second opening: a narrow flap through which food could be shoved in.

There were slugs suckered against the damp and traces of rats' droppings on the fetid straw.

Oveda lay down and began to cry, unconscious of the bugs that came out to investigate his body.

# *Chapter Four*

The Gringos left Revuelta at dawn.

The air was grey, not yet heated by the rising sun; still cold, though promising warmth when full light burst through the clouding mist of the false dawn.

Onslow rode in front, slumped down in his saddle with a black stormcoat buttoned tight against his throat, his hat shining silvery with moisture. The Mauser and the Colt were hidden inside his coat, but his right hand stayed close to the stock of the Winchester rifle, the model of 1895 with the box magazine, slung in the scabbard on the right side of his horse.

Jonas Strong came close behind, the Remington shotgun canted over his chest, his dark face impassive so that nothing showed behind the squinted eyelids.

Then Jamie Durham. Slumped down with his body letting the horse make the movements, a leather patch covering the bad side of his face.

And Yates McCloud. Still not convinced of the mission, but conscious of the money pressing against his belly like a comfort from the cold of the early morning mist.

Four men with a mission near enough to hopeless that all they had was hope. And a trust in their own ability to do the impossible.

Villa had given them ammunition and supplies and explosives. They were slung across the backs of the two mules he had thrown in, both of them good, sturdy animals, solid-backed and fast enough to keep pace with the horses they rode. Which was just as well, for Santa Granada was around one hundred miles ahead: at least a week through the uplands of central Mexico.

And Onslow had agreed to meet Villa in León. With Juan Oveda.

The country east of Revuelto was mostly barren hills. The ground climbed up in a series of bare ridges that only got covered with shrub and brushwood when they hit the high water plain, where more luxuriant foliage took over.

It was an empty landscape. Not only because of the terrain, but mostly because of the war: the villages that surrounded the railroad – mostly depending on it for their livelihood – were deserted. Either cleaned out by *federales*, or simply deserted in the face of an encroaching horde that frightened the inhabitants enough that they chose to give up their homes and hide, rather than chance a meeting with the Villistas.

The first night out from Revuelto the Gringos camped in a skeleton of a village, all lonely houses with windows shuttered like the coins on the eyes of a corpse. They slept in a deserted church; not much of a place, but better built than the other houses.

In the morning, as the sun broke through the mist, they moved out towards the high ground surrounding the village.

Onslow was in the lead, so he was the first to see the flutter of light off metal from the high ridges.

He slowed his horse, letting Jonas Strong catch up with him.

'You see it?' He asked. 'Sun off metal?'

'Twice.' Strong nodded. 'Two at least, probably more.'

'Tell the Kid and McCloud,' said Onslow. 'Tell them to be ready.'

'Sure.' Strong eased his pony back, letting it fall into line with Jamie's and McCloud's, dropping back until he was behind the mules.

No one said much, nor gave any sign of knowing there was an ambush – maybe – ahead.

They just got ready.

Onslow went on plodding up the slope, leaning forwards in his saddle like a man tired by the ride at the same time as he lifted the Mauser from the shoulder holster and snapped the hammer back. Jamie Durham settled the leather patch covering the left side of his face tighter in position and eased the Colt's Thunderer clear of the holster, letting the gun rest loose against his right thigh. Yates McCloud shrugged his jacket off of his back and draped it behind his saddle; then he reached over to scratch his armpit. As his hand dropped down, it flicked the safety thong loose of the Colt's Lightning and snapped the hammer back.

Jonas Strong reached down like a man scratching his hip. And cocked the Colt Automatic holstered on his waist and snapped the safety into place. Then, casually, he eased the Remington shotgun forwards, where his right hand rested naturally on the pistol-grip.

No one spoke.

There was no need: they were a team. Each man knew what to do.

Knew how the others would react, and thus knew how he should handle it. If it came to a fight.

Knew how to kill. In unison, or individually; but mostly that one thing: how to kill.

Fast and deadly.

Better than most men.

They went on up the slope.

Waiting. Anticipating.

Almost anxious for the killing.

And a rifle shot rang out like a bugle in the bright light of day.

The bullet was aimed at Onslow, and had he not been anticipating the ambush it would have struck him dead centre of the chest. As it was, he sensed as much as he heard the detonation, and shifted in time. He snatched the reins over, producing a squeal of protest from his horse as the head was dragged round to the left and the rider went clear of the saddle.

The trail was narrow here, steeply inclined and bordered on either side by heavy undergrowth. Onslow let go the reins as he crashed into a clump of bushes, rolling over so that he ended belly-down amongst the roots of a scrubby pine tree. The horse shrilled some more as fresh shots rang out, and spun round in its own length, lifting to a gallop back down the slope. The gallop ended abruptly as a rifle bullet struck the neck. The animal's head plunged suddenly downwards, and the front legs folded as though they had hit a trip wire. The hindquarters went on pumping so that the downwards momentum spilled the horse over itself, throwing it in a cartwheel along the trail.

Jamie Durham was already out of the saddle, hauling his own mount tight against the bushes, holstering his Colt and replacing the handgun with the Winchester. Directly behind him, Yates McCloud cursed as a shot whistled past his head and lunged clear of his own animal as the dead horse writhed to a stop across the path directly opposite his position.

'Leave 'em go!' Strong yelled. 'I'll take 'em!'

The two mules were linked to the Kid's and McCloud's horses by ten-foot leads, they were stamping irritably, not yet panicked as the horses, but still ready to run. The Negro got down on the ground – at the end of the line, he was to some extent protected by the angle of the trail, so that he could tether his own mount and catch the others as they came down towards him. He grabbed McCloud's bridle and manhandled the pony off to the side, looping the reins about the base of a bush. Then he dragged the mule up close, shortening the drag rope until he had sufficient in hand to halter the beast.

'Jamie!' he shouted. 'I'll take yours.'

The Kid swung the pony round and batted the stock of his rifle against the rump. The horse took off down the slope, dragging the protesting mule behind it. More shots crashed from up the ridge, and Strong came out at a run, setting his weight on the bridle as he turned the horse and dragged it alongside McCloud's. He hauled the mule in after, and then moved out past the overhang.

'Jonas?' Onslow was slotting the holster-cum-stock against the butt of the Mauser. 'I'm going up on the left side. Match me right.'

'Yo!' Strong began to clamber through the bushes.

'Jamie! Yates! You cover us.' Onslow peered up the rise, estimating distances. 'Give us fifteen minutes, then you start moving up.'

The Kid shouted, 'Yeah! You got it.'

McCloud said, 'Shit!' quietly, then: 'Sure.'

Onslow moved out. The slope was steep here, the trail angling slightly to the right before curving round to make a straight ascent to the rim. The upper level was thick with trees, roots thrusting out where the final edge cut starkly from the ground. Mostly it was all brushwood with clumps of pine occupying the shallow bowls where soil had gathered. It was difficult to climb, because the angles of the slope were steep and the bushes presented a near-impenetrable barrier, and he was holding the Mauser in his right hand, using his left to haul himself upwards with the aid of knees and toes and elbows.

McCloud and the Kid were laying down a solid wall of covering fire. The flat cough of the Kid's Winchester was punctuated by the sharper crack of McCloud's Colt. And from up the slope there came the angry crackle of answering gunshots.

Onslow estimated at least five men.

All armed with rifles.

Mostly Winchesters, with maybe a few Carcanos. Three at the most.

He reached a bank of sheer dirt with roots sticking out like tentacles, and began to work his way along, to the left.

After a while the bank gave way to a slope of shale that spread in a broad fan towards the lower ground. Onslow scrabbled round the overhang and began to work his way up to the rim.

He reached it with sweat dripping into his eyes, and paused for a moment, catching his breath. The rifles were still firing from his right, and McCloud and the Kid were still answering from down the slope. He stood up, estimating that something like ten minutes had gone by, and moved forwards through the trees.

Jonas Strong was slower getting up. As best he could tell, whoever was mounting the ambush thought Onslow must be dead. At least, most of the fire seemed to be directed in his vicinity, which made climbing difficult.

He shifted wide over the slope, ignoring the problems of the near-vertical frontal assault in favour of working out to the right so as to come up on the riflemen from the flank. Halfway up he triggered his shotgun at the sky and let loose a mighty scream. Then he reloaded and moved silently along the ridge. The ruse seemed to work, because the fire shifted round to focus on McCloud and Jamie.

He went on climbing, his wide lips spread in a broad grin.

Onslow moved through the trees, the Mauser held against his chest, stock snug against his arm, forefinger on the trigger.

He came to a clearing and halted. There was a circle of trees surrounding an area of open grass, partially covered with small blue flowers. Around the far side, the flowers were crushed down, and from over beyond the trees a horse snickered softly.

He swung round the clearing, looping out to the south so that he was finally moving back to where the rim of the ridge overlooked the curve of the trail. The staccato bark of McCloud's pistol was still counterpointing Jamie's Winchester, and the answering fire was still crackling from the rim.

He moved in closer. There were six horses tethered amongst the trees. Beyond them there were six men.

Two wore the grey jodhpurs and matching tunics of *federales*. They held Carcano rifles. The other four were dressed in a mixture of outfits that ranged from white cotton to concho-studded pants and fancy waistcoats. They all had at least one sidearm, some wearing double belts, and they all carried Winchester rifles.

Onslow waited, slanted sideways behind the bole of a big pine tree, until he saw Jonas Strong moving in from the left side. Like his own, the Negro's approach was hidden under the crackle of gunfire.

He waited until Strong was in close, then waved his left hand.

The Negro saw the movement, dropping to a crouch with the Remington shotgun pointing ugly as an open grave in Onslow's direction. Onslow waved slowly, gesturing for silence. Then pointed at the men spread along the ridge. Pointed at Strong, and waved him in. Pointed at himself, and then at the right hand end of the line.

Strong nodded.

Onslow grinned and stepped out from the trees.

He lifted the stock of the Mauser to his shoulder, clutching the underslung magazine as his right forefinger clamped down on the trigger. The automatic pistol barked like a dog in heat. It bucked against his shoulder as the spent shells ejected from the topwards loading gate. 7.63mm bullets sprayed a series of bloody fountains from the backs of the men on the ridge.

And Jonas Strong came in with the Remington blasting ought-ought gauge shot at the bodies.

Onslow's first spray ruptured holes from the ambushers' backs. Two men died as the lead slugs shattered their spines and ripped through their bodies to puncture hearts and lungs. One screamed as his elbow shattered, thrusting a twisted remnant of his arm out in front of his face. And then Strong's shotgun blasted a cloud of thunder over the ridge.

The man nearest the discharge was turned sideways as his shirt stripped clear from his body and his ribs showed through the tatters of wasted flesh. The man beyond him screamed as his left eye got pulped and half his face sprayed away.

Strong pumped the Remington and went on squeezing the trigger. And Onslow went on firing the Mauser. One of the *federales* twisted round onto his knees. He had dropped his rifle and was raising a Luger in Onslow's direction.

Onslow held the trigger of the Mauser down. And the 7.63mm slugs exploded into the *federale*'s chest. The magazine was almost empty, but that made little difference: the man was already wounded, bleeding from two holes in his back that were suddenly joined together on the wake of the bullets exiting from his body. The grey tunic covering his chest indented, the material getting dark as blood spurted from the holes. Then the rear fluttered out on a swathe of gouting red that was flecked through with shards of bone and sickly-glistening streamers of body matter. The *federale* went backwards, pushed by the Mauser. He dropped his Luger as he got shoved over the rim of the ridge, his eyes staring sightlessly at the hot and empty sky.

He slid down the slope, then hit a bush and came to halt. Ridiculously, his left foot tangled in the branches so that he hung upside down, mouth gaping as blood flowed over his eyes, bubbling from his mouth and nostrils. It washed over his face and dripped onto the ground, slow and sticky, attracting flies and ants. Like a memory of a life.

Onslow dragged a fresh clip of cartridges from his vest and fed them into the gate of the Mauser.

Strong came out from the trees with a Colt Automatic in his hand. There was a man moaning, not yet quite dead, despite the bullet holes in his side and the massive destruction of the scattergun. Strong looked at his face and then at Onslow. Onslow nodded, and the Negro squeezed the trigger, ending the man's agony with a single shot that plunged a hole through his brain and ended all the pain.

McCloud and the Kid came over the rise.

'What the hell was that about?' asked the Southerner. 'Why'd they try to ambush us?'

'We was there, I guess.' Onslow dismantled the stock and fitted it back on the carrying harness. 'Just happened to be us coming up the trail.'

'Maybe not.' Strong pointed down the ridge. 'Look.'

Too far distant to permit the identification of individual details there was a column of horsemen moving slowly towards them. There were seven riders, bunched close together.

'What the hell?' McCloud shaded his eyes with his hat. 'You think this crow-bait was waitin' for them?'

'Looks likely,' murmured Onslow. 'What you think, Jonas?'

The Negro shrugged. 'Not much else to wait for up here. It ain't exactly a main highway.'

'I wonder why,' mused Onslow. 'What'd be so special about them?'

'You gonna wait an' ask?' demanded McCloud. 'Or do we do the sensible thing an' get the hell out?'

'They're a hour off yet,' said Onslow. 'We'll be long gone.'

'So let's get the horses,' said McCloud, 'and get gone.'

They went back down the ridge and took the animals up to the rim. Onslow stripped his saddle and gear from the dead animal and slung it on a mule. Up on the rise he transferred it to one of the ambushers' mounts, a big bay gelding. While he was doing that, McCloud was busy with the dead men's saddlebags.

'Looks like they was travelling light,' he said. 'There ain't nothing here, except these.'

Triumphantly, he lifted two full bottles of tequila. Onslow thought about smashing them, knowing how the Southerner got when he was drinking, but then decided it wasn't worth the chance of a stand-up fight. Instead, he said: 'All right, Yates. But go easy on it.'

'Spoils of war, major,' grinned McCloud. 'Spoils of war.'

He stowed the bottles in his own bags as Strong and Jamie unsaddled the riderless horses and turned them loose. Then the four Gringos mounted up and continued southwards.

Not one of them gave the dead men a second thought. That kind of sudden, pointless firefight was the kind of incident that happened in a country ravaged by a bloody war. Huerta's men enforced a savage rule over the land they occupied, taking little notice of the law they claimed to uphold. And the vicious attacks of the revolutionary forces were directed at the single aim of destroying as many of Huerta's troops as possible in the headlong drive for Mexico City. Neither side took much time out to consider the problems of the *peons*, with the result that large numbers fled the fighting only to return to burned-out farms, fields wasted by shell fire. And some chose not to stay to rebuild. After all, if some army was going to destroy a lifetime's work, why not follow its example? And to a *peon* who had never even heard of Carranza or Pancho Villa, to whom Mexico City was a fable, everyone was an enemy. The land was filled with bandit groups: displaced farmers, deserters, the scavengers who followed any army.

In Onslow's mind the killing was justified completely enough that there was no need to remember it, even. The six men had opened fire without provocation: they had paid the dues of the attack.

But one thing still nagged at his mind. The trail he was riding was deliberately obscure. There were faster and easier routes south. He had chosen this one because it was little used; because there were – by now – enough *federales* in Mexico who would recognize the Gringos. And know that the four men promised a huge reward. So the trail he had chosen in consultation with Villa was a quiet one, not used by many other than hunters.

Not promising any profits to lurking bandits.

So why had the six men been waiting?

And who were the riders behind? Why had they, too, chosen this obscure path?

The thought went on gnawing in his mind, and he reined back, letting McCloud take the lead as he fell back in pace with Jonas Strong.

'You wondering what I've been wondering?' asked the Negro. 'Like why an ambush? And why that column behind us?'

Onslow nodded. 'Could be worth checking. You want it?'

'Sure.' Strong grinned. 'Tonight. They won't see me in the dark.'

# *Chapter Five*

The terrain south of the ridge was flatter, but denser with vegetation. The sunwashed foliage of the lower slopes gave way to thick stands of exotic undergrowth so that they rode with the constant problem of low-hung branches and trailing vines. The air even this late in the day was warm, humid, and rich with the scent of flowers.

Onslow called a halt when they struck a shallow pool fed by a natural spring. The surface of the water was thick with the wide-spread pads of water lilies, so that it was necessary to cut the plants away before it was possible to find clear water. The pool was banked with rock, heavy with a green moss that glowed phosphorescent under the moon, the sides further covered by trailing roots that hung down into the water like gnarled tentacles. All around, a heavy canopy that blocked out most of the moon and hid their fire, there were heavy-fronded trees.

They watered their animals and cooked up a mess of beans and beef. McCloud poured tequila.

Jonas Strong ate the food and drank one mug. Then he stood up, casual, and saddled his horse.

'Where's he going?' McCloud drained his fourth mug. 'What's goin' on?'

'Checking the back trail,' murmured Strong. 'Just making sure no one interrupts your drinking, Yates.'

'Good boy.' The Southerner laughed. 'Nice to see . . . friends,' he adjusted his words quickly when he saw Strong's face, 'looking out for one another.'

'Yeah,' said the black man. 'It must be.'

He got up on his horse and rode out into the night.

It was close on midnight before he struck the ridge, and when he came out into the clearing behind the scene of the would-be ambush coyotes ran snarling from the bodies. Down the trail, not far from where the first bullets had hit there was a fire burning. It was mostly hidden behind the overhang of the ground, but there was still sufficient glow showing against the blue-black sky and the pine trees that Strong was able to locate the place.

He tethered his horse to a tree, and wrapped a bandanna about the muzzle. Then he went forwards on foot, working his way slowly – cautiously – down the slope until he was one hundred yards from the glow of the flames.

He got down on his belly and eased forwards with the cut-down shotgun clutched in his hands, wriggling through the bushes with his breath coming in slow, soft whispers and his eyes scanning the darkness ahead. He halted a spread from the fire and circled round: there were no scouts out, so he went back to his original position and moved in closer to where he could see and hear the camp.

It was located inside a fold of the ridge, shaded on the south side by tall walls of sandstone that shone blood-red in the fire glow, on the other sides by over-hanging *piñons*.

The cut was filled with sand. Stupid, he thought, if they were trying to hide: sand reflected light too much, and their fire was built up too high to think the trees would shade it. Besides, it was giving off too much smoke. That could be smelled, and even against a dark sky, grey showed over blue.

He got up against the overhang and looked at the people inside the hollow. They had their horses penned off at the far end. Which was fine for protection – unless some attack came in from above – but not much use if anyone wanted to make a fast getaway. There were no guards on the upper level: just two Mexicans leaning back against the entrance to the split with Winchester carbines in their arms and cheroots in their mouths. Giving off tell-tale red glows.

Around the fire there were five people.

They were eating better than the Gringos: the smell that drifted up to Strong was the succulent odour of pan-fried steak. And really good coffee. And whisky.

One man had grey hair. Almost silver in the moon's light. He seemed to be in charge. Four of the others looked like ordinary *vaqueros*. They wore sidearms: mostly Colts, with Winchester rifles in the scabbards of the saddles behind them.

The last one seemed odd. Not built like the others, nor armed the same way.

It took Strong a while to realize that it wasn't a man at all, but a woman. Dressed up to look like a man.

It was not until she took off her hat that he realized her sex, for her hair was pinned up on top of her head, and the loose-fitting coat she wore covered her breasts as effectively as the tight pants she wore.

Strong watched a while longer, then slithered back through the undergrowth and worked his way silently back up the lift of the ridge.

He found his horse and got up on the saddle, cantering back to the pool.

Jamie Durham was on guard when he came in, swinging a rifle in Strong's direction as the Negro called, 'It's Jonas. All right?'

'Move in,' said the Kid. 'Slow. So I can see you.'

Strong came in slow, and Jamie said, 'Jonas! What you see?'

'Tell you in the morning,' said Strong. 'It's real interesting.'

He got down from the saddle and took his pony over to the water. He felt weary and excited at the same time. But mostly he felt like sleeping.

Dawn brought the chatter of parakeets through the brightening mist around the pool, and Strong woke. Onslow was already shaved and dressed, brewing coffee on a small and smokeless fire. Jamie was shaving, taking care to hold the scarred side of his face away from the others, and McCloud was groaning, bleary-eyed, as he doused his head in the water.

When they all were hunkered around the fire, sipping coffee and chewing bacon, Onslow asked Strong what he had seen. Strong delivered a succinct report that brought a frown to Onslow's face.

'What the hell's a woman doing out here? Dressed like a man?'

'We could wait up an' find out.' McCloud's face got pasted with a lecherous smile. 'It's been a long time since I . . . '

'Pulled trouble on us.' Onslow's voice cut the Southerner short. 'Don't go lookin' for it again, Yates. Not on our time.'

'Shit! That was a mistake,' grunted McCloud; sullen. 'A misunderstanding.'*

'That was trouble,' snapped Onslow. 'What we want to avoid.'

He reached over to his saddlebags and pulled out a map, hand-drawn.

'Look,' he traced the line of their route, 'we don't know where they picked this trail up, but now they're on it they can't do nothing but follow it. The next settlement's this place. Tapara. If they catch up there, we'll take a look at them. But that's all.'

Tapara was five days' distant.

Five days spent crossing country that alternated between semi-jungle and ridges of high timber that gave onto arid, near-desert terrain. They held to as fast a pace as was possible without winding the horses, and by the time they reached the place their supplies were almost gone.

It wasn't much of a place: just a spread of adobe houses built around a stream that ran through the centre of a

*See: THE GRINGOS no.6 – MAZATLAN.

stone-walled bowl. None of the houses stood taller than one level, and the whole village had about it an air of lazy resignation. Onslow dragged binoculars from his saddle and focused in. There was a stone bridge spanning the stream, the houses stretching out maybe two hundred yards either side, and a few more back. There was a church, the arch holding the bell making it the tallest structure there; a cantina; a store of some kind. There was no sign of government troops.

'All right,' he said. 'Let's go in.'

They went down the ridge, looking hard for signs of danger.

Nothing happened, and when they came through the flanking shacks to the open space around the bridge the only person watching them was an old man chewing a melon slice in the shade of a wall. He smiled as he saw them, and waved a greeting. Strong waved back.

They crossed the bridge and halted outside the cantina.

'Jonas, wait here.' Onslow swung down. 'Yates, Jamie, you come with me.'

Without waiting for an answer he went inside the saloon.

It was dark, the windows shuttered against the noonday heat, the air thick with the smell of *chorizo* and pulque. Down at the far end a rough counter displayed food that was blurred by the movement of the flies. Tables and chairs, cut rough with axe and adze, filled the centre. To the right there was a stone-and-plaster bar with a fat man behind it making a pretence of polishing earthenware mugs.

McCloud and the Kid wandered down to the far end, glancing at the food as their eyes flickered around the room for sign of a second door.

Onslow went up to the bar.

'*Hola.*' The barkeep set down the mug. '*Americanos*, no? *Quieren* whisky?'

'*Tienen* whisky?' asked Onslow.

The barkeep laughed, shaking his treble chins. 'No,

*señor.* I got some very good tequila, and the best pulque in all of Potosi.'

'Tequila,' said Onslow. 'How come it's so quiet?'

'This godforsaken war.' The man set three mugs on the bar and reached down to fetch a stone flagon out. 'All the young men have gone to fight.'

'Who for?' Onslow asked, dropping a coin. 'Which side?'

'Side?' the barkeep shrugged. 'What do sides mean to people like us? The people here are farmers, *amigo.* They grow food to eat. If they have any left over, then they sell it. And after they sold it, they come in here to spend their money. There are no sides for a farmer; just the land.'

'So why'd they go?' Onslow reached for the salt and lemon before he chanced the liquor. 'Why are they fighting?'

'The *federales*, may they all rot in hell.' The barkeep spat on the floor, pinning a cockroach long enough that he was able to crush it. 'They came here a month ago. They said there was a battle to be fought and all the young men had to join the army of that bastard Huerta. They took all they could find and shot two who said they wouldn't go. Jesus Vizcaya and Saldano Brigada. Jesus had a mother with the coughing disease, and his father lost his right hand a year ago when a tree crushed it. Saldano never had a father and his mother vomits blood all the time. So the *federales* shot them. After that, the other young men went off to find Pancho Villa.'

He poured himself a drink, licked up salt and lemon, and tossed it back in one.

'Stupid war! Both sides take our young men. And when it's over not many will come back, so the only people who win anything are the politicians down there in Mexico City. And they won't do anything for this town. Which will rot away without men to tend the fields, so no one will come here, and I shall become poor.'

'Travellers?' asked Onslow. 'What about them?'

The barkeep laughed. 'Travellers? Since the *federales* there's been no one but you. No one comes to Tapara.'

Onslow nodded, turning as McCloud and the Kid joined him. McCloud shook his head as he reached for the tequila, and said, in English: 'No other way in.'

'You want to eat?' asked the barkeep. 'I can fix you a nice chilli. I got a girl, too. Young. Guaranteed clean.'

'Now that,' said McCloud, 'sounds interesting.'

'We ain't staying long, Yates.' Onslow stared hard at the Southerner. 'Nor making no trouble.'

'After this time,' said McCloud. 'I ain't takin' long. Besides, we got to get supplies, an' as you're the man with the travel money, you'll be busy a while.'

'The horses could use a rest, major.' Jamie sounded nervous. 'So could I.'

Onslow saw the hand scratching at the Kid's arm and knew what he meant.

'All right. We'll stop over one night.' He emptied his glass. 'No more.'

The food was bad. The chilli was mostly grease and beans with only a few chunks of meat thrown in, and all through the meal McCloud drank tequila and opined what the girl would be like. When they were finished they stabled their mounts and the mules behind the cantina and arranged to sleep on the straw. McCloud laughed at the thought of spending a night in a bed while the others still slept rough.

Onslow and Strong spent the afternoon purchasing fresh supplies while Jamie and McCloud stood guard on the horses.

Tapara stayed empty. A few old women came out after the siesta time and ambled around with nothing much to do except stare at the two men and the shuttered church. Much later some old men came out onto the boardwalks and sat, slapping cards down or whittling on wood, or just sitting, as they discussed the amazing event of four *Americaños* coming to Tapara.

Onslow and Strong got back to the stable with loaded

sacks. And found McCloud halfway drunk on tequila, and Jamie Durham starting to show all the signs of his addiction.

'I'm sorry.' His face was drawn and pale; at least the side they could see beyond the mask. 'I gotta do it soon. It's been a long time.'

'Sure. Go ahead.' Onslow nodded. 'You got the stuff?'

Jamie grunted an answer, raising the oilskin pouch in which he kept his needles and his dope. Onslow and Strong got McCloud on his feet and walked him back to the cantina.

Jamie watched them go, grateful of the privacy. He went to the far end of the stable, where drying grass was piled up in two empty stalls. He climbed into the farthest and peeled back his sleeve. Then, taking great care not to spill anything, he wound a thin rubber tube around his left bicep and tugged it fast. When he braced his arm the veins stood out like pitted gulches. He took a syringe from his kit and struck a match, sterilizing the needle in the flame, then shaking out the fire and spitting on the head before tossing it loose of the hay. His hands were beginning to shake as he took the vial of clear liquid from the pouch and punctured the cap with the needle. They got steadier as he withdrew the plunger, watching the column of the hypodermic fill with morphine. Then he clenched his left fist to make the veins stand up and stuck the needle into an open space.

He didn't even feel the pain of the prick.

Just watched the plunger go down, pumping the drug into his body.

And set the hypodermic carefully back inside the pouch and very carefully wrapped the flaps round and tied the strings before setting it all back in his saddlebags.

And then he stretched back against the warm hay and closed his eyes.

. . . Sometimes there was a good dream. It might be about his father's farm, where the aspens and the willows grew thick along the creek that covered the bottom land. And

Mary would be waiting for him there. Golden hair shining through the sun-dappled shadows as the brook whispered behind. And she would kiss him. And they would sink to the ground, her dress sliding suddenly from her body so that Jamie, too, was naked, and they would touch. Gently.

And make love. Gently.

Lovingly.

. . . and sometimes it was bad.

And Mary would be floating face-down in the crick. Her hair would be spread in a golden fan around her head. And she would roll over as the little darting fishes played amongst her hair, and her yellow locks would drift down to reveal the empty eyes and the grinning stumps of the teeth.

. . . and sometimes it was 1910. And Mary was clapping, cheering him on as he mined the pass the Mexican bandits had to use to get back home. And he was proud – the youngest corporal in the Army Engineers – knowing that he was doing good work. Knowing that the mines he set were right. But the bandits had taken another route, and the Engineers had had to go down to defuse the mines.

And then the dream ended in worse pain.

Ended in light and darkness. Like a mine going off in a man's face.

. . . and sometimes, now, it was just colours and sound, the one translating into the other. So that the smell of the hay became a mellow symphony of distant flutes, and the snuffling of the horses was swarming brown; the pungent odour of manure a stark yellow that was superseded by the heat, that was warm gold. Far off, the clack of harness became dancing sparks of silver as the smell of the horses was a solid line of bass fiddles.

. . . And Jamie Durham went down into the morphine sleep that kept him alive. And forgot about the world and the troubles it had given him. And forgot about everything.

'Someone better check him,' said Strong. 'Besides, we got all those explosives back there.'

'Not me,' said McCloud. 'I got an appointment.'

Strong started to say something, but Onslow spoke faster.

'I'll watch him. You get some sleep, Jonas. And you, Yates. Remember we're leaving early.'

'Yessir!' McCloud stumbled to his feet, mocking a salute. 'I'll try to remember, *sir*.'

'You better.' Onslow stood up. 'Else I'll whip the arse off you.'

'*Sir*.' McCloud repeated. 'At your pleasure, sir.'

He wandered off down the bar, stumbling from side to side with his glass slopping tequila over the floor.

'Come on,' said Strong. 'Come on, major. Best to let him work it off.'

'Yeah.' Onslow nodded. 'I guess.'

They went out to the stable behind the cantina and checked the horses and the mules and Jamie Durham. In that order. The horses were all bedded down with plenty of food. So were the mules.

Jamie was sound asleep. He hadn't eaten anything since mid-day, but he didn't seem to need much when the drug fever took him, so all they did was stow his kit back in his saddlebags and cover him with a blanket. Then Jonas Strong curled up on a pile of fresh hay and went off to sleep. Knowing that Onslow was awake somewhere in the stable with a Winchester in his hands and a Mauser and a Colt Automatic to back the first gun up.

Yates McCloud mouthed his tequila down his throat and asked the barkeep where the girl was.

The fat man smiled and said, 'There is a question of the money first, *señor*.'

'There's a question,' answered McCloud, 'of seeing what I'm payin' for.'

The barkeep smiled some more and said, 'Give me five *yanqui* coins now. The girl is waiting for you. I told her about you, so she's ready. If you don't like her, you can have your money back.'

'Christ Jesus!' McCloud slammed money across the stained top of the bar. 'She better be good. Or I come back for that.'

The barkeep smiled and said, 'Second door down the alley. There's a light outside.'

McCloud nodded and went out through the curtains.

The night was high-country cold, and the town empty as a graveyard at midnight. He went down the boardwalk and stepped into the dust of the alley beyond. There was a single candle burning over a plank door. It was held inside a glass funnel, with enough wick and wax to keep it shining all the night.

He knocked on the door.

And got a surprise when it opened.

## *Chapter Six*

The pistol sticking hard against McCloud's stomach was a .45 calibre Colt's Peacemaker.

The hammer was all the way back, so that the only thing holding the gun off of firing a cannon hole through his belly was the hairy finger on the trigger.

McCloud looked at the gun. Then looked at the hand. Then looked up into a pair of dark brown eyes that were smiling like the ice on a winter pool.

The door opened wider, and a hand reached out to clutch his coat and haul him inside the shack. Behind him, the door got kicked shut and he was in darkness with fingers moving over his body, lifting his own gun free of the holster and checking his body for other weapons.

Then someone said, 'He has nothing more.'

And a match got struck, and a lantern was lit.

And McCloud saw a silver-haired man and a brown-haired girl seated on a narrow bed that was sunk in at the centre with the efforts of past customers.

'I think I come to the wrong place,' he said. 'I was looking for a lady.'

A pistol shoved up against his ribs. Hard. And the man with the silver hair said, 'No, *señor* McCloud, you came to exactly the right place. I wanted to talk to you.'

'Who the hell are you?' McCloud was horribly conscious of the guns pointed at him. 'What you want with me?'

'My name is Alvaro Raza.' It was said as though McCloud should know instantly what it meant. 'My daughter is Carmen Raza. That answers the first part of your question.

For the second. Well,' he motioned to the single chair, 'sit down.'

Prodded by the guns, McCloud sat down.

'I need help,' said Raza. 'That is the second part. From you.'

'Me?' McCloud shrugged. 'How can I help you?'

Raza chuckled. '*Señor* McCloud – that is your name, isn't it? – you are one of the men the *federales* and the Villistas call The Gringos. *No es?* The others are a man called Cade Onslow who once served with the Army of the United States, and a Negro sergeant called Jonas Strong. There is a third, called Durham, who wears a patch on his face to hide the wounds he got when a bomb exploded. You are the fourth man in the team. *No es?*'

'You know one hell of a lot about us,' admitted McCloud. 'How come?'

'Like you, Yates, I have made money knowing what people do. And where to find the right men.'

McCloud got an ugly feeling that he had been suckered into a trap. And maybe the others along with him; though that part didn't worry him so much.

'You said you wanted help,' he said. 'What kind of help?'

Raza shrugged. 'I have aided the Huertistas and the Villistas. I am a businessman, after all. But the *federales* confiscated my ranch, and after that it was difficult to live in Durango, so I have chosen to go south. Exactly where does not concern you. What does, is that I have friends in León. Also that I will pay you each five hundred dollars American to help me get there.'

'All of you?' McCloud hadn't yet grasped the size of the offer.

'No,' said Raza. 'Just Carmen and myself.'

He was speaking English now, so he ignored the *vaqueros* watching the doors.

'I will pay off my men. They are no better than cowboys,

anyway. And pay each one of you Gringos five hundred dollars.'

'There's a battle coming up there,' said McCloud. 'You sure you don't want to go someplace else? I could take you.'

'I am sure you could,' said Raza. 'But I want to go to León. And I want to be sure I can get there. Listen, *hombre.* If you hadn't been ahead of us on that trail we'd have been killed. These men with me aren't fighters, they're *vaqueros.* I need killers. Like you.'

'I'll have to tell the others,' said McCloud. 'Ask them what they think.'

'You do that,' said Raza. 'Tell them about the five hundred dollars, too. And tell them I have friends in León.'

'Sure.' McCloud nodded. 'I'll do that. Right now.'

Raza gestured at the men holding the pistols on McCloud, and the Southerner was allowed to stand up. He went out through the door and hurried down the street. He was three quarters of the way along before he remembered that he hadn't even seen the Indian girl.

But now she didn't seem to matter so much.

'Listen,' he said to Onslow, 'it's worth five hundred bucks each on top of what we're doing already.'

'And extra trouble,' said the older man. 'Escorting a *hacendado* to León. Him and his daughter.'

'Might be cover.' Strong spoke for the first time. 'Yates could have a point. They could be watching for us. But would they watch for five men with a woman in tow?'

'And he knows people in León,' McCloud added. 'That could be useful.'

'I guess I'm outvoted,' said Onslow. 'All right. Bring him up, Yates. I'll talk to him.'

Jonas Strong got hidden down behind the bars of a stall with his scattergun pointed out in front as Onslow checked the load on his Mauser and placed himself behind the doors. And McCloud went to fetch Raza.

When the Mexican arrived he refused to step into the stable.

Onslow gestured for Strong to come up to the front as he stepped out between the doors with the Mauser angled on Raza's belly.

'I only want to make a deal,' said the Mexican. 'I can prove my honesty.'

He tossed a sack onto the ground separating him from Onslow.

Strong came out to pick it up, holding the Remington on the *vaqueros* flanking Raza. He took it back to the stable and counted the money inside.

Then: 'Yo! Like he promised.'

'Why?' Onslow kept the rapid-action gun pointed in Raza's direction. 'Why us?'

'You're the best,' said the Mexican. 'And I need the best.'

'And you know people in León?' queried Onslow. 'How?'

'I have friends everywhere. That's how I know about you,' said Raza. 'How I know you can get us there. Why I trust you.'

He waved his own men back and motioned for Onslow to come forwards. The American stepped closer, angling the Mauser tight on the Mexican's stomach.

Raza looked down at the narrow muzzle and smiled.

'I might help you get inside Santa Granada.'

'How?' Onslow's finger tightened on the trigger. 'How'd you know that?'

'Friends,' said Raza. 'In both cases.'

'Why?' Onslow demanded.

Raza shrugged. 'My own reasons, *señor* Onslow. Do they matter if we can help one another?'

Onslow thought for a while. He was used to making snap decisions, and he couldn't think of any reason a Mexican landowner would bring his daughter into the firing line without a good reason to support mercenaries he knew were fighting for Villa.

It didn't matter that he couldn't rightly figure out why. Just that Raza was prepared to spend five hundred dollars American for each man. A total of two thousand.

Enough to guarantee his need.

'All right,' he said. 'You got a deal.'

'Good,' said Raza. 'Excellent. When do we leave?'

'Send your men off in the morning,' said Onslow. 'We'll stay over one more day. Then leave at dawn.'

'Thank you,' said Raza. 'I like a man who makes fast decisions.'

'One thing,' Onslow added. 'You foul us up, and we dump you. Understood?'

'Alive, or dead?' asked the silver-haired man. 'Do we have a choice?'

'Depends,' said Onslow. 'On how it happens.'

'I hope it doesn't,' answered Raza. 'Not that way.'

# *Chapter Seven*

In the mornings a bell rang one hour before dawn. Juan Oveda couldn't hear it, not from inside his cell, but the changing shift of guards made sure he was awake. They came down the corridor thudding their rifle butts against the doors, and if a face failed to show at the window, then they opened the door and kicked the prisoner to his feet.

Soon after that, Oveda got a mug of bad coffee and a bowl of mouldering beans. Once a week there was a bucket of water placed inside his cell and he was allowed to wash before slopping out the floor. Every second week, he got fresh straw – at least, it was fresh by the stinking standards of his imprisonment.

He was bug-bitten, rancid, and half-blind when *Coronel* Alcaza had him brought out into the daylight. His pants stank of the uncontrollable flushings of his bowels brought on by the putrid diet, and his beard was stretching halfway down his chest, thick with lice and straggling wet whcre he regularly sucked the final remnants of the beans away. He blinked in the sun light coming in through the windows.

'Sit down,' said Alcaza. 'Please.'

The invitation was followed by a rifle blow that thudded a butt into Oveda's kidneys and sent him stumbling into the chair.

He doubled over, gasping, as a cold, dry voice said, 'I think he's going to puke.'

Alcaza gestured at the guards standing behind Oveda, and one left the office, returning with a bucket that he placed under Oveda's chair.

'If you throw up, pig,' he said. 'Do it in that. Or you lick it up.'

Oveda nodded, wiping bile from his mouth onto his beard. Then he squinted his eyes at the men behind the desk.

Alcaza he recognized from his induction to Santa Granada. The other man was a stranger: a *yanqui*. He was tall and thin, dressed in a white suit that came close to blinding Oveda. He had white gloves on his hands and dark glasses covering his eyes. His thinning hair was cropped short, to a stubble over his head, so that everything about him was white. Except the glasses.

'Listen,' he said. 'My name is Hiram Bender. I could get you out of here right now.'

'How?' asked Oveda; not trusting the man.

'Easy,' said Bender. 'You just tell me about Valdaña and sign a confession about how Carranza is working with Villa to overthrow the legal government.'

Oveda blinked some more, his shuttered eyes gradually adjusting to the unusual light. And shook his head.

'I don't know Villa.'

'That doesn't matter,' said Bender. 'Does it?'

'Carranza doesn't like Villa,' muttered Oveda. 'He thinks he's a bandit.'

'He is,' said Bender. 'Isn't he?'

'I don't know.' Oveda shook his head again. 'He was, I suppose. But now? He's a revolutionary hero.'

'He's a bandit,' said Bender. 'Always was. Always will be. You want to see Mexico run by bandits?'

'No. Nor by tyrants. Like Huerta.'

A rifle stock slammed against his back, smashing him from the chair. He surged forwards, too weak to lift his arms in anticipation of the fall. So his face struck the desk and he felt a tooth shatter loose. Spat blood, feeling his head spin.

'Pick him up and get out.' It was Bender who spoke. 'Don't hurt him.'

Oveda was dimly aware of being picked up and set back in the chair.

Of a solicitous hand applying a silk handkerchief to his bleeding mouth.

Of someone offering him water, and lifting the bucket so that he could spit his blood and his broken tooth into the puddled vomit.

'You could finish all this,' said Bender. 'Easily. Just do what I ask.'

'What's that.' The way Oveda's mouth was damaged it came out as *Wash At.*

'Here.' Bender set a sheet of paper on the desk and put a pen in Oveda's hand. 'You sign that.'

'Can I read it first?'

'You don't need to.'

'What does it say?'

'It says that Carranza sent you to negotiate a deal with Huerta. Because he was afraid of what Villa and Zapata might do to the country.'

'He is,' said Oveda. 'But he didn't send me to do anything like that.'

'Does it matter?' asked Bender. 'The fact is there, isn't it?'

'Not the deal with Huerta.' Oveda dropped the pen. 'Never.'

'Why not?' Bender leant over the desk, his dark glasses only inches from Oveda's face. 'If Huerta and Carranza signed a treaty, then the United States would back both of them. Together, they'd wipe Villa and Zapata and all the other bandits clear of Mexico. Think about it! Huerta and Carranza together. Backed by the U.S. of A. Stable government, plus a guarantee of American support against rebels.'

'I can't convince Carranza,' said Oveda. 'He's committed to fighting Huerta.'

'But if you signed this,' said Bender, 'then Carranza might think again. He listens to you. And you could persuade him to make a treaty. It could end the war. See Carranza in power. See you out of jail.'

'And America would govern our country?' asked Oveda. 'Put Huerta and Carranza in power like two men driving the same coach?'

'That's better than the war,' said Bender. 'Isn't it?'

'No,' Oveda shook his head. 'That would be one driver pulling to left while the other pulls to the right. You can't drive a coach – or a country – like that.'

'So what do you suggest?' Bender's voice got cold. 'Give it up to Villa and Zapata? Give it to bandits and peasants?'

Oveda shrugged. 'Better than Huerta. Better than America.'

'You're crazy,' said Bender. 'You want to rot in prison?'

'I won't sign away my beliefs,' said Oveda. 'Not for your curious arguments.'

'You'll change your mind,' said Bender; quietly. 'I promise you.'

He turned to Alcaza and nodded. The Mexican pressed a button on his desk, and outside the room there was the long trilling of an electric bell. Then the door opened and two guards came in. They both carried rifles. They fetched up in salute position behind Oveda's chair. Snapped hands to their hatbrims, and clicked their heels together.

Then one swiped his rifle round so that the stock slammed hard against the left side of Juan Oveda's jaw and the man pitched clear of the chair for the second time. The guards picked him up and dragged him, heels-down, from the room.

There was a time of pain.

In a curious way, it was almost better than the total boredom of his cell.

Until the torturers set all their ingenuity to work.

They began by beating him. Four or five men pounding at him with fists and boots. He lost several teeth, and his nose and three ribs were broken. But he survived.

And he still refused to sign Bender's document.

So they began to try more sophisticated methods.

They pressed cigar butts to his feet. Held him face down in a tub of freezing water that still held remnants of the ice cubes used to chill it, until he was choking with his mouth wide open and his eyes bulging clear of his skull. Then they pressed the cigars against his testicles. And when that didn't persuade him to sign, they inserted a rubber hose into his anus, and pumped a gallon of boiling water inside his bowels.

By then Oveda had learned how to beat them.

It was not easy: the easiest thing would have been to sign Bender's document, and chance going free. Though he doubted he ever would: it was more likely that he would be killed, and Bender would say that he had chosen to flee abroad.

So he chose the other path.

One side had to be stronger, but physical strength was not necessarily the right way: there were times when weakness could win.

So, after the torture, when he was at his weakest, he kept himself moving. He paced his cell. He did press-ups until his chest heaved and his body ran with sweat. Then he masturbated. Over and over, until he was weak from it. Then forced himself upright and began to pace the cell again.

So when they took him out each morning and each afternoon, he passed out quickly; too weak to suffer the pain for very long.

And after a while they gave up: the victim was beginning to punish the torturers.

They put him on a work detail.

*Coronel* Alcaza himself came to supervise the move.

'You are going to cut rock until you die,' he said. 'You are stupid: it might have been so easy for you.'

'No,' said Oveda. 'That would have been harder.'

'*Tonto!*' Alcaza spat into the cloying dust. 'I'll see you dead. I'll laugh on your grave.'

'People like me,' said Oveda through his broken teeth, his voice whistling, 'might reach up to bite your foot.'

Alcaza hit him with the silver-studded butt of his quirt, and turned away. And Juan Oveda was herded off to where the prisoners of Santa Granada chipped stone from the rock until they died.

And that was where he met Ramon Cortez again, and began to think about escape.

# *Chapter Eight*

The Gringos left Tapara in the cold light of early dawn.

Cade Onslow took the lead, with Alvaro Raza alongside; Yates McCloud and Jamie Durham herding the mules; and Jonas Strong bringing up the rear with Carmen Raza.

'Why you doing this?' asked Onslow. 'Why take the hard way?'

'Shouldn't you have asked me before?' replied Raza. 'Before you took my money?'

'I guess,' said Onslow. 'Maybe I forgot. It don't make no difference to what I promised, but I'd like to know.'

'I trust you,' said Raza. 'So I'll tell you. Thinking you a man of some honour, I do not believe you will kill me for what I say.'

'Sounds real interesting,' said Onslow. 'Tell me more.'

'I own a lot of money.' Raza smiled. 'Not the kind that is easily taken: it is mostly invested. In Mexico; everywhere. When the *federales* took my ranch there was a young captain. A man called Raul Montes. He wanted to take my daughter, too. Neither Carmen or myself approved of the idea. Anymore than we approve of some Villista raping her.

'So: we came south. There would be little love for a man of my kind in the north, and as I told your friend McCloud, I know people in León. Given enough time, I can arrange to travel abroad. To England, or France. Maybe even Spain.'

'So why,' asked Onslow, 'did you choose to travel with us?'

'Don't you see the simplicity of it, *señor* Cade?' Raza chuckled. 'The moment Pancho Villa reaches León the banks will cease to exist. If Villa's bandits find anything there to rob it will be because the fleeing Huertistas have forgotten to take it with them. But you will get there first. So I shall have time to arrange for Carmen and myself to transfer our money to the coast. To Santa Cruz, perhaps, and take a boat to Europe.'

'I could stop you,' said Onslow. 'I could take your money.'

'You wouldn't,' said Raza. 'That would disgrace your honour. Besides; you couldn't: it all needs my signature. And I can give you more help than money; for your cause.'

'Yeah?' asked Onslow. 'How?'

'I have contacts in León,' said Raza. 'They can help you get into Santa Granada. And out again.'

'You best tell me,' said Onslow. 'I'd like to hear how.'

'Soon enough you will,' said Raza. 'In a while.'

They rode on through the high country of central Mexico, the early haze giving way to a grey, cloud-filled sky that threatened rain. After the sun rose and burned off the mist, the rain came. A thin drizzle at first, but then a steadily thickening downpour that plastered the horses' manes against their necks and turned the track into a churning sea of mud. The riders pulled slickers clear of their saddles and shrugged inside the enveloping stormcoats, turning the collars up high against the trickle of water that fell from their hats.

They moved forwards through a grey mist as impenetrable as the dawn vapours. The rain was warm, near as hot as a steam bath. It puckered the trail ahead and hid the road behind; the droplets spanged off the heavy fronds of the exotic trees like gunshots exploding in the distance, causing them to jump in their saddles with hands reaching down to their guns before they realized it was just the sound of nature washing the earth clean.

After three hours of riding thoroughly wet through the curtain of water, Onslow called a halt.

There was a place along the trail where the trees came down tight enough that slickers could be draped over the branches to fashion a makeshift tent. Onslow and Strong spread theirs over the limbs, while McCloud and Jamie hung shades down either side.

'Isn't that dangerous?' asked Raza. 'How can you see who's coming?'

'No one comes up this trail,' grunted Onslow. 'Not unless they're waiting for someone.'

'Yeah,' said Strong. 'Like planning an ambush.'

Which reminded Onslow of what he should have asked the Mexican before they started.

'How come that ambush was waiting?' he said. 'It must've been for you.'

Raza looked embarrassed. 'I don't know. I suppose word got out.'

'Of what?' McCloud moved into the talk. 'Ain't no six bandits gonna lay up for a rape. Not even with so pretty a target as that.'

Carmen Raza blushed as he ducked his head in her direction, and turned away.

'There's gotta be something else,' said McCloud, standing up. 'Suppose I take a look at your horses.'

Raza opened his mouth to say, 'no', but by then McCloud was out into the rain and rummaging through the saddle bags.

After a while the others heard him whistle and shout, 'Christ Jesus! You ain't gonna believe this.'

'What?' Onslow asked. 'What won't we believe?'

'This!' McCloud came back under the makeshift tent with water dripping off his face and two solid blocks of gold in his hands. 'I'm holding close on a lifetime's work. And there's six of the same out there.'

'So?' said Onslow. 'What you suggesting we do, Yates?'

'Hell! You need to ask?' The Southerner thrust the bars close against the older man's face. 'Look at these bright, beautiful hunks of life insurance. I know gold, Onslow. So

I know each one of these is worth around four thousand dollars. And there's eight of them! That's thirty-two thousand dollars. Split that four ways, it means eight thousand dollars apiece. Don't you see it?'

Onslow reached a cheroot from his vest and struck a match. He took a long time lighting it. And when he was done, he turned to Raza.

'Why'd you trust us to take you through? With that much gold along.'

Raza shrugged nervously. 'Like I said: you are the best. I thought I could trust you.'

'Yeah,' said Onslow. 'That's right.'

'What you mean?' asked McCloud. 'With eight thousand dollars a head, we could all get set up someplace. Jesus! We got the money Villa gave us, plus the Mex's five hundred, and now this!'

He turned around, holding the two gold bars.

'Don't you see? All we gotta do is take it. He won't even miss it much. The bastard's rich! He'll go on to León an' pick up more money there. An' we'll be heading for the coast. Living high.'

Onslow shrugged and looked at Jonas Strong. 'What you think?'

'Ain't my money,' said the Negro. 'Never did like taking what I never earned.'

'Jamie?' Onslow turned to the Kid. 'How do you vote?'

'That's a whole lotta gold,' said the youngster. 'But I thought we agreed to help these people. I never thought robbing folks was helping them.'

'You're crazy,' said McCloud. 'All of you. Jesus! Leave 'em their horses and let's go. Now! With the gold.'

'We made them a promise, Yates.' Onslow's voice was calm; conversational. 'We made a deal with them.'

'Fuck that!' said McCloud. 'That was a deal made before we knew what they was carrying.'

'Still a deal,' said Onslow. 'We took their money and gave our word.'

'I don't see that.' McCloud dropped the gold bars into the centre of the tent. 'Way I see it, they tricked us. That gives us the right to hike the price up.'

As he said it he reached down under his coat, hauling out the Colt's Lightning with the hammer back and the muzzle pointed on Onslow's chest.

'That's crazy,' said Onslow, not moving. 'How far d'you think you'll get?'

'With thirty-two thousand dollars? Sorry.' McCloud corrected himself. 'With thirty thousand: I'll leave those two bars for you. A long way. A long rich way.'

The sound of Strong's scattergun lifting up took his eyes away from Onslow.

'How far, Yates?' asked the Negro. 'How far you think this ought-ought could throw you?'

McCloud laughed. 'You fire that in here, boy, an' you'll kill yore boss and most everyone else. You want that?'

'I don't,' said Jamie Durham. 'I don't want none of it. Forget it, Yates.'

While he was speaking he lifted his own Colt to point on McCloud's chest. The hammer was all the way back, and his forefinger was tight on the trigger, only his thumb holding the pistol off of planting a .41 calibre slug through McCloud's body.

'Jamie?' McCloud sounded confused. 'I figgered you to be coming with me.'

'No,' said the Kid. 'Not now, Yates. I learned something better than taking the main chance.'

McCloud stared at the youngster, then down at the Colt's Thunderer in his hand. Then over to Strong's Remington and across to the Colt's Automatic Onslow had drawn and cocked while he was talking.

'Jesus!' he said. 'You are all fucking crazy.'

'Maybe we are,' said Onslow. 'But right now, you take the gold back to where you found it. You want to take your money and run, then you're welcome. But it's the last chance, Yates. The next time you try something like this, you're dead. No second chance.'

'Shit!' said McCloud. 'You're all crazy.'

But he went outside with the two gold bars and put them back in the saddlebags.

And Alvaro Raza said, 'Thank you. Gentlemen.'

Onslow said, 'Shut up.'

The rain lifted after a while and they set off again, following a trail that was now thick with mud and pelted by the dripping water falling from the trees. They rode slower, Onslow in the lead with Raza and his daughter behind him; then Jamie Durham and a surly Yates McCloud. Jonas Strong brought up the rear.

An hour before nightfall they came on a deserted village and made camp inside what was left of the walls of an adobe house. Nothing inside the village stood taller than five feet, and down what had once been the main avenue, there were the deep craters of shellmarks. The buildings were pocked with the acne scars of machine gun fire, and where the church had once been there was just a shell with a solid oak door at the front and nothing behind.

There was a skeleton pinned to the door. It was still supported by the bayonets thrust through the hands, held up by the bleached finger bones and the tatters of cloth still remaining about the remnants of the body. There was a crucifix thrust down through the gaping mouth so that the base had ground against the bones behind the throat. It hung there, leaning out of the empty jaws with the sun casting its shadow in tandem with the patterns of the bones.

There was no way of telling which side had killed the priest, nor even if his own parishioners had turned against him.

So they left him there and made camp inside the best of the houses, and cooked up a mess of lamb and beans with the girl tending the pot while her father passed round a bottle of good American whiskey. The horses were inside the building, sheltered in the only other room, where they could get out fast over the broken wall.

Onslow called off a guard rosta, giving McCloud the first watch. He went out with the Southerner.

'Yates.' He emptied his mug and set it down on the window ledge. 'We need to talk.'

His tone was casual, pitched low enough that the people inside wouldn't hear him. McCloud nodded, starting to grin as he misinterpreted Onslow's gesture that they move away from the house.

'Sure thing, major.' He cradled his Winchester in folded arms. 'You changing your mind?'

'Something like that.' Onslow led the way past the house to where an alley ran down from the flanking building. 'Let's get out of earshot.'

'Now you're talking.' McCloud's grin got wider. 'I reckoned you'd see sense in time. Hell! We'd be crazy to kiss that much money goodbye. Jesus! all we gotta do is take it. The Mex won't scarcely notice it's gone – way he talks, he's loaded. When do we do it?'

'Now,' said Onslow. And hit McCloud hard in the mouth.

The blow came up from around his belt, powered by all the weight of his leanly muscled body. It took McCloud on the left side of his jaw, jumping his mouth open and spinning his head sideways. A cut appeared on the lower edge of his lip. Onslow followed with his left hand, driving it forwards with the fingers stiff, into the Southerner's belly.

McCloud groaned and doubled over, catching the Winchester as it tumbled from his opened arms.

'Time we sorted this out, Yates.' Onslow stood back as McCloud fought to suck air into his lungs. 'I taken enough crap from you. I seen you drunk an' I seen you sober, an' it's hard to say which way you're worse. But you gotta learn one thing: we're a team. We work together, and the only way we can do that is if all of us stick together.'

'Which means taking orders from you,' wheezed McCloud. 'Ain't that right, *major*?'

'That's right,' said Onslow. 'Just like the Army.'

'Fuck the Army!' snarled McCloud. 'Fuck you!'

And he came up with the Winchester lifting to point on Onslow's belly, the lever snapping down to drive a shell into the chamber.

Onslow took one step forwards, pivoting on his left foot as his right came up in a high kick that struck McCloud's right hand where it was fastened through the underslung lever. The Southerner gasped, his hand jumping free with blood running over the knuckles. He let the movement turn him so that his left hand stayed tight on the barrel as Onslow turned sideways, leg lifting over and down from the kick.

McCloud transferred his grip, settling both hands around the barrel of the carbine as he brought it round, club-like, against the older man's side.

He swung it hard, smashing the stock against the area between Onslow's ribs and belt. Onslow gasped, still off balance from the kick, and staggered back. McCloud spat blood from the side of his mouth and reversed his swing, angling the stock at Onslow's skull.

Instinctively, the brown-haired man ducked, lifting an arm to fend off the blow. It smashed against the underside of his left arm, numbing his hand and bringing a fresh gasp of pain from his mouth. McCloud grunted, and brought the carbine round to drive the butt hard into Onslow's belly. Onslow tried to cover the movement, but was too slow: it rammed into his midriff and sent him pitching back, doubled over with bright lights sparking across his eyes.

Dimly, as if in slow motion, he saw the Winchester curve round again. And felt pain burst through his skull as a blow that seemed to jar his brain loose of the cranium threatened to smash him off his feet.

He went down on his knees, shaking his head as he spat blood and tried to clear the lights from his eyes. He sensed, rather than saw, the carbine lift up as McCloud swung the gun over his head, preparatory to bringing it down in a sweep that would mash Onslow's skull.

Onslow rolled to the side, letting instinct take over as he curled his body and rammed both feet out against the Southerner's ankles.

The butt of the Winchester slammed into the dirt at the same time as Onslow's thrust hit McCloud's legs. McCloud's feet went out from under him and he teetered forwards, letting go the carbine as he put out his hands to break his fall. Onslow curled onto his face.

Got his knees under him, and pushed halfway upright.

McCloud shifted onto his left elbow, right hand reaching for the fallen gun.

Onslow came over with a bunched fist swinging round to drive down against the exposed neck. And McCloud grunted like a pole-axed steer and went flat on his face in the dust.

Onslow got up on his feet and kicked the Winchester clear. There was the sticky feeling of warm blood on his cheek and in his mouth, but the spinning of the world was slowing down and now he could see through the lights inside his mind.

'Stand up, Yates,' he said. 'We need to settle this.'

McCloud curled over, shaking his head as he braced his body on toes and hands. Then he powered forwards, driving his head into Onslow's stomach. Onslow saw the move coming, and took it like a matador accepting a dangerous charge. As McCloud hit him, he folded at the waist, bringing a knee up at the same time as he linked his hands and brought them down against the back of the Southerner's neck. The cap of his knee hit McCloud on the point of his jaw, and the secondary action of the down-swinging hands twisted the head back. Had Onslow applied a little more power, then McCloud's neck would have been snapped. As it was, the double blow merely stunned the Southerner, who wrapped both arms around Onslow's legs and went on pushing until Onslow was pitched off balance.

McCloud grabbed hold of a foot and twisted, reaching up to angle the pressure of knee and ankle against one another.

Onslow raised his other leg and pounded the heel of his boot against McCloud's shoulder and neck until the grip fell away.

Both men rolled back in the dust.

McCloud spat blood. His face was filthy; a caking of dirt and sweat and blood plastered his face. His teeth were black with blood, and he was panting heavily.

Onslow wasn't much better. There was a steady run of crimson dripping into his moustache, combining with the grime there, and the left side of his face was flaring into a livid purple bruise.

They stood up.

McCloud took a swing with his right hand. Onslow blocked it, and hit the Southerner in the chest. McCloud gasped and kicked Onslow hard in the right knee, following through with a left-handed punch that smashed against Onslow's eye, closing it. Onslow feinted left and hit McCloud in the mouth, then drove three hard punches into the man's belly.

McCloud doubled over, and Onslow swung his foot up in a kick that should have connected with the Southerner's face and ended the fight.

But McCloud grabbed his foot and lurched back, hauling him off balance.

They both went down again. Onslow tugged his foot clear and kicked McCloud in the ribs with the other boot. McCloud rolled over and lifted up to drive his head against Onslow's groin. Onslow yelled. And took hold of the Southerner's ears, twisting them as he forced the butting head back. McCloud reached up, trying to break the grip. And Onslow lifted both knees against McCloud's chin and then hit him twice on the upper point of the cheekbones.

McCloud's head jumped to right and left.

His eyes closed as a fist swung lazily in Onslow's direction. And he slumped face-down in the dirt.

Onslow stretched back, panting. There were bells still

ringing inside his skull, and he could taste blood inside his mouth.

Whatever else anyone said about Yates McCloud, he was a mean street fighter.

Onslow waited, grateful of the pause, until the Southerner opened his eyes again and got up on his knees.

'You understand now, Yates?' he asked. 'You take my meaning?'

'I guess,' said McCloud. 'Yeah, I do.'

'Next time,' said Onslow, 'I'll kill you.'

'Have to, I guess.' McCloud picked up his carbine and blew dust from the action. The blowing left splatters of blood on the metal. 'Need to.'

'Don't let it come to that,' said Onslow.

'We'll see,' said McCloud. 'Not this time. But maybe later. Some other time.'

'Yeah.' Onslow picked up his hat and dusted himself off. 'But not now.'

# Chapter Nine

Outside the Hotel *Placido* in León there was a big, black car. It was a cause of wonderment to the children and the older citizens, because they had never seen a car of that size or type before.

The mayor had a car – a small brown machine with a funny French name that no one could pronounce right – and the garrison commander sometimes appeared in a pale grey automobile that spluttered, and shot clouds of gas from the exhaust pipe; like a heifer in heat.

But this was something different.

It was enormous. Big as a water tank, and quiet when it moved. It shone, too; thanks to the efforts of the man in the dove-grey uniform who came out to polish it each day. He came out exactly three hours after dawn every morning, just before the sun got hot. And he applied wax to the coachwork and polish to the metal, so that the solid hubs shone brilliant silver as the sun lifted over the plaza, and the black body gleamed, reflecting back the rays that began to strike into the centre of the town. He washed the tyres, too, and scrubbed all the dust from the windows. And the few children daring enough to peer inside could see that the seats and the walnut panels of the sides and frontage were as gleaming clean as the outside.

The man who did all this said nothing to anybody, except to the skinny *Americano* who gave him orders. Though why a man who wore a shoulder holster with one of those big American automatic pistols strapped under his left arm should take orders from a sickly-white person like that, no one who watched could understand. But when the white-faced *yanqui* beckoned, then the other went running. And that was when the little boys clambered up over the running boards of the Packard, and left sticky finger marks on the polish, racing away as soon as a *federale* – or, worse, the chauffeur himself – appeared.

'It's not working.' Hiram Bender filled two glasses with brandy. 'It's all going wrong.'

The chauffeur took the glass. He would have preferred a beer, but he didn't argue with Bender. Few people did. He didn't speak, either, knowing that his boss would get around to saying what he meant in his own time.

'Villa's taken Lagos.' Bender swallowed liquor. 'He took the place like a falling apple: easy as knocking it off a rotten tree. He's grouping to come here now.'

'That's rough country,' ventured the chauffeur. 'Even with trains.'

'They'll cross it,' said Bender. 'Villa won't hold up longer than it takes him to refuel and rest his men. Besides, Obregon's moving in from the west. And Zapata's got Huerta buttoned up to the south. It's a losing battle.'

'So what do we do?' The chauffeur saw that Bender's glass was empty, and moved to fill it. 'We can't go north. Not with Carranza in control.'

'I know that,' snapped Bender. 'I think we've got a month. Maybe six weeks. It'll take Villa that long to bring the trains down. He'll know how strong the defences are here, so he'll most likely wait a spell before he attacks.'

'And then?' the chauffeur asked. 'What happens then?'

'León falls,' said Bender. 'What do you think? The garrison won't hold up against Villa. That's why I wanted Oveda to come out in support of Huerta. Dammit! that way at least we'd have had a bargaining point.'

'And now?' the chauffeur asked. 'What do we do?'

'Get the car fuelled up,' said Bender. 'Load as much

gasoline as you can. I think we're going to Mexico City. Be ready.'

'Yessir!' The man in the dove-grey uniform put down his glass and settled his cap on his head. 'I'll do that.'

Bender watched him leave the room as he thought about the *mestizo* girl who occupied the small cubicle on the ground floor. The *patrón* had said she was half Yaqui. Interested in whitemen.

He went over to the door and swung it open, shouting after the chauffeur.

'Send that girl up!'

'Yessir!' The chauffeur cursed under his breath and folded the five dollar note he was holding back inside his jacket. 'Straightaway, sir.'

Juan Oveda dropped his pick into the pile that was guarded by two troopers with Mannlicher rifles, and fell into line.

Ramon Cortez fell into step beside him.

Both men were weary. Their breakfast had been tacos and beans; both mouldy. And they had been working all day with only a half hour break when a second issue of beans was distributed. From six in the morning until noon, they had been quarrying rock. The same from thirty minutes after noon until sundown. Oveda was gulping air like a drowning man. His hands were bloody where the pickaxe had scoured callouses and blisters into his fingers. And he thought he was dying.

Cortez was a little better. Not much, but enough to make a difference.

'Listen,' he whispered. 'When you're stronger, we'll get out. We'll club a guard and run for the hills.'

'How far do you think we'll get?' asked Oveda. 'The guards have guns. And they patrol the hills. We need a better plan.'

'Think about it,' said Cortez. 'We'll talk it over tomorrow, *si*?'

'*Si,*' said Oveda. '*Mañana.*'

And he followed the prodding of the rifle butts – because by now the guns had no faces – and went down to his cell where the cockroaches scrambled over his food that he ate without thinking and went to sleep on the stinking straw oblivious of the insects and the rats crawling over his body.

That was how it was in Santa Granada: a man survived.

That was all.

If he didn't, he died: a simple equation.

Onslow woke up to a high, bitingly cold morning.

There was frost on the ground and frost on his face, he thought. Then he realized it wasn't frost at all, but the crusting of blood from McCloud's blows.

He rolled clear of his blanket and splashed water over his face. It washed the blood away, but his body still ached. He swilled out his mouth and spat the last remnants of the fight away.

'Here.' Jonas Strong handed him a mug of coffee. 'Drink it.'

Onslow swallowed a mouthful and shook his head. 'Yates?' he asked.

'There.' Strong pointed at the far side of the building. 'I carried him in after you done with him.'

Onslow lifted up enough that he could see McCloud covered by a blanket, his snores bursting little globules of blood round his nostrils.

'Me and Jamie brought you over,' said Strong. 'Both of you. You damn' near killed one another.'

'It was in my mind,' admitted Onslow. 'I thought to do that.'

'I think he learned the lesson,' said the Negro. 'Maybe you did, too.'

'Maybe,' said Onslow. 'I don't know.'

'I sure hope Yates did,' said Strong. 'For all our sakes.'

'Shit!' said Onslow. 'We need the bastard to keep Jamie

with us. Yates knows how to find things you or me wouldn't know where to start looking.'

'I guess,' said Strong. 'That's probably right.'

'You think there's another way?' Onslow asked. 'Without Yates?'

'The Kid's not using the drug so much now.' Strong shrugged. 'He's depending more on us than on Yates. An' that Southern mother makes trouble every time.'

'But we're still a team,' said Onslow. 'Jesus! That was what I told him last night.'

'You're the boss, major,' said Strong. 'You give the orders.'

Onslow laughed, wincing as the cuts on his mouth cracked. 'That's what I told McCloud. Cover my back, Jonas: I got a feeling Yates is still greedy.'

'You got it,' said the Negro. And turned back to the fire.

By the time they quit the deserted village the sun had come up and started to burn the cold off the land. The trail south wound up through a series of high country ridges that climbed steadily upwards towards a massive canyon that was marked on Onslow's map with the warning words: *Indios!*

Villa hadn't said much about this area, never having penetrated so far south. And Onslow knew nothing at all about it, so that the only information he had had come from a *dorado* who had once ridden down to Mexico City. The man had said that the country was empty – which was so far mostly true – except for Indian settlements.

Onslow's experience of Mexican Indians was limited to brushes with renegade Apaches riding out of the Sierra del Norte, and the odd bunch of Yaquis. His plan was to ride around the canyon and push eastwards, then south.

At least until the first arrows struck his horse.

They went in through the neck and chest, bringing the animal down in a heaving line that pitched him over the dropping head to spill him on his face in the dirt. He tasted blood in his mouth and rolled over, snatching the Mauser clear of the shoulder holster as the whistle of fresh arrows got hidden under the rattle of answering gunfire.

He saw McCloud go down with an arrow in his left shoulder. Then saw the Southerner lift up with the Colt's Lightning blasting flame against the trees, firing right-handed as he stumbled clear of his horse and got bellied down on the trail. The pony ran clear, halting where Onslow's animal blocked the trail. And then arrows made a pincushion of its body and it went down in a welter of flailing limbs and spurting blood.

Strong's shotgun blasted upwards against the slope. The range was uselessly far, but the sound of the ought-ought gauge shots going off gave Alvaro Raza time to spring clear of his horse and drag the animal down the slope of the down side trail. At the same time, Jonas Strong heeled his pony back and lifted out of the saddle with his hands dragging the reins over and down so that the animal got turned in its own length and fell over its own feet to crash sideways across the path a hundred feet back from Onslow's position.

In between, Jamie Durham lifted his Winchester from the saddle boot and came down with his horse between him and the attacking Indians. He let the horse run free as he snatched Carmen Raza from her saddle and swung her over to the side of the trail. Then he bellied down, with his Winchester pointed up at the attackers. The girl screamed as he dropped her into the cover on the far side of the trail, and Jamie clamped a hand over her mouth.

'Stay quiet,' he said. 'Don't tell them where you are.'

Carmen nodded and he took his hand away.

'You know how to load a gun?'

She nodded again, and he said, 'Good. You can load for me.'

Onslow's Mauser went off with a high-pitched rattle, the 7.63mm slugs shaking leaves from the trees above.

'Yates!' He shouted. 'You all right?'

'No! Goddam it! I'm hurting,' yelled the Southerner. 'I'm hit.'

Onslow moved out from cover and ran to where McCloud was stretched in the dirt. He reached the Virginian and pointed the fresh-loaded Mauser up into the trees, loosing off a fresh load of shells that shattered branches without hitting any of the hidden Indians. The clip sprang clear of the upwards gate, and he snatched it out, replacing it with a fresh load. Then he hooked his left arm under McCloud's chest and dragged the Southerner to his feet.

'Can you walk?'

'I guess,' said McCloud. 'I hadn't thought much about it.'

'Hell!' said Onslow. 'See if you can run.'

They stumbled back into the cover of the trees flanking the road. Onslow looked at the arrow sticking out of McCloud's shoulder.

'That's not too deep,' he said. 'I'll take it out.'

Before the Southerner could answer or argue, he yanked the shaft free.

'Why?' asked McCloud. 'What you do that for?'

'We're a team,' said Onslow. 'We need each other. Stay still.'

He peeled McCloud's jacket and shirt off, ignoring the arrows that were still answering the fire coming from Strong and Jamie and Raza. The arrow had gone in on a shallow trajectory, most of its force lost where it struck the Southerner's clothes. The actual wound was little more than a prick into the skin of McCloud's shoulder.

'You'll live,' said Onslow. 'We'll clean the wound later.'

'If we get away,' said McCloud.

'We will,' replied Onslow. 'I ain't getting stopped here. Not by bronco Indians.'

He reloaded McCloud's Colt and put the gun in the Southerner's hand.

'Listen,' he said. 'I'm going to talk to the others. When you see me move over, you start firing.'

McCloud nodded, and said: 'Sure. Major.' There was no inflection on the word, not this time.

Onslow moved over to where Raza was pointing a Colt's .45 Peacemaker up the slope and said, 'Keep firing when you see a target.'

Raza nodded, and Onslow moved on. He explained his strategy to Jamie Durham and Jonas Strong, then shifted back far enough along the trail that he was able to clamber up the slope behind where the Indians were placed. He worked slowly through the trees, taking his time as the sun faded over the hills, waiting for the light to strike from the west.

When it hit the eastern face of the ridge, and he knew where the Yaquis had settled into position, he moved down the slope.

There were four Indians.

They were spaced out along the line of the trail, holding to the high ground where they could fire down on anyone moving along the old roadway. They all held bows, with the arrows tipped into the ground beside them. Two carried pistols in Mexican Army holsters on their belts.

Onslow put the Mauser down on the warm grass between the trees. Then he lifted the holster clear of the shoulder rig and snapped the pistol's butt into the mountings that ran down the holster-stock.

He lifted the automatic pistol to his shoulder, sighting down the barrel.

And squeezed the trigger.

The gun went off with a stark clatter. Shells sprayed clear of the release gate as he traversed the muzzle across the line of Yaquis, emptying the thirteen shell magazine against their backs.

The first Indian jerked back on his knees as the bullets hit him just above the belt that separated his breech-clout from his rawhide shirt. He thrust his arms out, letting go of his bow as blood plumed from his spine and stomach while the bullets mashed bitten bones into pulped kidneys.

The second man turned as he heard the ugly chatter of his death reaching towards him. He opened his mouth in time enough to take slugs through his gaping jaws so that they pulped his voice down into the fragmenting bones of his throat, mashing his tongue and teeth back against his windpipe even before the whole system blew clear of his neck.

The third and fourth Indians were luckier: they were lifting up on their feet, so that Onslow's bullets hit them both across the belly.

They were stitched by the slugs, the ugly lead bullets rupturing their stomachs with sufficient force that they were both doubled over and hurled backwards. Blood wept from their bellies, and larger goutings erupted from the holes in their backs. They got tumbled over the slope, somersaulting downwards with their bows flying clear of their dead hands and their lives emptying behind them.

Onslow fresh-loaded the Mauser and went down the slope.

Jamie Durham was bringing Carmen Raza out from the trees, and Jonas Strong was hauling the mules up. Alvaro Raza was shaking his head as he came out onto the trail, and Yates McCloud was dragging himself up, with his right hand pressed to his wounded shoulder.

'Yaquis,' said Raza. 'The worst kind of Indians: they'll prey on everyone. On anyone. Thank God you were here.'

'Yeah. I appreciate that vote of confidence,' said Onslow. 'There's just one small problem, though: We lost two horses.'

He pointed up the trail to where his own mount had died and McCloud's had run clear.

'So now,' he said, 'we fetch up double.'

'We still got the mules,' said Strong. 'They're all right.'

'I ain't riding no mule,' said McCloud. 'That's a nigger's mount.'

Strong laughed: 'So walk, white boy.'

'Ride it,' said Onslow, irritably. 'Or we part company. Here and now.'

His voice got flat and hard as McCloud started to complain, and the innate differences between the two men began to boil surfacewards again. The Southerner was grinning, confident that Onslow would not leave him wounded, standing with one hand pressed against his shoulder. There was a moment of silence as Onslow's brown eyes caught and held McCloud's blue. Onslow's fingers touched the butt of the Colt Automatic.

'Major!' Jonas Strong's voice echoed loud. 'Don't!'

'He won't,' sneered McCloud. 'Not yet, at least. Not while I'm wounded.'

Onslow's teeth ground together as he realized that the Southerner was right: he still retained sufficient honour to refuse shooting a wounded man.

Or he was too soft, he thought.

Raza broke the stand-off. In a perfectly matter-of-fact voice, he said:

'The Yaquis usually poison their arrows. Even a flesh wound can kill.'

McCloud's face went pale, and he turned from Onslow to stare at the Mexican.

'You're lying!'

Raza shrugged. 'Time will tell, *señor* McCloud. But the truth may be unpleasant for you.'

'Jesus!' McCloud twisted his head to peer at his shoulder. 'We gotta do something about this.'

'We?' asked Onslow. 'Why *we*?'

'Christ!' McCloud took his hand from his arm as though afraid the poison might spread to his fingers. 'You can't leave me. Not poisoned.'

'Get up on the mule,' said Onslow. 'And keep your mouth closed.'

McCloud nodded and let Jamie Durham help him astride the mule. Onslow boarded the second pack animal, and they took off down the trail, wary of a follow-up attack.

Several miles farther on, where the trail wound around a curve of bare rock, they halted. Beyond the curve there was a cleft in the hillside, a vee-shaped notch that was protected on two sides of the vee by sheer flanks of naked stone, on the open end by a shale-covered drop that went down forty or fifty feet to a shallow stream. They halted their mounts at the centre of the vee, and Jonas Strong climbed to the head with his Winchester while Jamie mounted guard on the northern trail. Raza and his daughter got a fire started as Onslow went down to the stream to fill their canteens.

McCloud had peeled out of his shirt by the time Onslow got back, and was staring at the wound. It didn't look very bad, even less lethal under close examination than when Onslow had seen it the first time.

'I think it should be cauterized,' said Raza; solemnly. 'A heated knife blade would take the poison out.'

'How heated?' asked the wounded man. 'How hot you mean?'

'Oh, red hot,' said Raza; equably. 'Then burned out with powder.'

'Christ!' McCloud produced one of the tequila bottles and took a long swallow. 'Get it done, then!'

'You're bein' real brave, Yates,' murmured Onslow. 'Real brave.'

He went over to where Jamie was leant against the rock. 'Borrow your knife, Kid?'

Jamie grinned and reached inside his belt: 'Sure. Hope it's sharp enough.'

Onslow chuckled and snapped the catch of the switchblade down, watching the slender, razor-sharp blade snap into view. McCloud was leaning back on a blanket that Carmen Raza had spread over the grass, letting the girl cushion his head as he gritted his teeth and groaned softly. It was hard to tell how much was fear and how much play-acting.

Onslow squatted down to thrust the blade into the flames. Raza joined him, holding the tequila.

'That true about the poison?' murmured the American. 'They really do that?'

'I don't know,' said the Mexican, softly. 'It just seemed like a good way to get him mounted.'

Onslow grinned. '*Seguro, amigo. Y gracias.*'

'*De nada,*' smiled the Mexican. 'I owe you more than that.'

'This'll do for now,' chuckled Onslow. 'I'm enjoying this.'

He stood up. The blade of the knife glowed a bright cherry red as he went over to McCloud.

'This is gonna hurt, Yates.' He hunkered down beside the Southerner. 'But it's for your own good.'

McCloud nodded, white-faced, and took hold of Carmen Raza's hand. 'Go ahead.'

Onslow grabbed the man's bicep and pressed the red-hot blade against the arrow hole. There was the sweetly acrid stink of scorching flesh, and McCloud groaned, this time not feigning at all. Onslow worked the point into the wound, turning the blade so that the whole cut was cauterized. Raza pulled a cartridge from his belt and bit the slug away, spitting it onto the grass. He passed it to Onslow as the American dropped the knife, and fetched a match from his vest. Onslow sprinkled powder over the cut and nodded. Raza leant across, touching the burning match to the grains.

McCloud yelped as the powder ignited and a flash of pale flame erupted over his shoulder.

'Sure hope that's cleaned it,' said Onslow. 'Sad thing, losing an arm.'

McCloud's face got paler still as a thin sheen of sweat glistened on his forehead.

'We'll rest up a while,' said Onslow. 'Give you time to recover. What you think, Raza?'

'Not too long.' The Mexican answered impassively. 'If there is poison still, then we shall need a real doctor. The nearest is in León.'

'Best get there fast as we can, then,' said Onslow. 'Soon as you feel fit to ride, Yates, you let me know.'

'God! I can ride now.' McCloud sat up. 'Let's go.'

'Wait up.' Onslow pushed him back, starting to bandage the wound. 'You gotta ride that mule, you know.'

'Sure,' said McCloud. 'That's fine. Where is it?'

'Waiting for you,' grinned Onslow. 'Real patient. I think you got something in common.'

## *Chapter Ten*

'Listen,' said Ramon Cortez. 'I have it all worked out now.'

'*Si?*' Juan Oveda spooned the thin gruel into his mouth and frowned his doubt. 'Tell me.'

Cortez glanced round at the guards. Three were huddled by the food wagon, their rifles propped against the wheel as they spooned beans into their mouths and passed a bottle between them. Two more were perched on the rocks above, hunkered down with Winchesters rested over their knees; waiting to be replaced, and get their chance to eat. The prisoners were sprawled on the sun-heated rock, spooning slop with the exhausted determination of men close to starvation.

'It has to be soon,' said Cortez. 'If we stay here much longer, we'll be too weak to try it.'

'Try what?' asked Oveda, not very interested in anything more than the greasy food. 'What can we try?'

'When the guards eat,' said Cortez, 'they put their guns down. Look.'

Oveda nodded. 'So?'

'So there are three rifles down there,' whispered Cortez, 'and only two above us. If some men ready to risk their lives were to take those guns, they could kill the men above us. They wouldn't expect an attack out here.'

'There are two men on the wagon,' said Oveda. 'They have guns, too.'

'Pistols,' snapped Cortez. 'And they're cooks. We could take them easily.'

'Maybe you could,' said Oveda, 'but I'm no fighter. I never shot anyone in my life.'

'You ever get tortured before?' asked Cortez. And when Oveda shook his head: 'You want it to go on?'

Oveda shook his head again.

'It's easy to learn,' said Cortez. 'Killing. You want something badly enough, you can point a gun at a man and pull the trigger. That's all.'

'I'm not sure,' said the Carranzista. 'I don't know.'

'They're enemies,' said Cortez. 'They'd kill you.'

Oveda looked up at the sky. It was wide and burning blue above the hills, and it gave him no answers at all. He felt his belly rumble – whether from hunger or the greasiness of his diet, he couldn't tell – and thought about the food he had eaten in Valdaña. With Maria.

Who was dead.

Who had been raped and murdered and left pinned to a tree like a scarecrow.

And the men clustered by the wagon wore the same kind of uniform.

'All right,' he said. 'Tell me what to do.'

'It's easy,' said Cortez. 'If we all work together.'

The plan had the attraction of simplicity. There were three ways a man condemned to Santa Granada might get out of the prison: the first was in a plain pine coffin when he died; the second was if someone broke him out; the third was if he broke out himself.

The first and second, Cortez either disliked or didn't believe in. So the third was his only way. And it made some kind of sense.

Each morning, soon after dawn, the prisoners were taken out under guard to begin chipping the rock. They worked until noon, when the food wagon arrived. By then the guards were feeling almost as hot as the prisoners. The distribution of food and water was a kind of amnesty, when the prisoners were considered too weary to do anything but eat and drink, and the guards took advantage to enjoy their own food. The men manning the wagon were old and fat, and the guards controlling the convicted men were complacent: accustomed to herding beaten prisoners too weak to protest.

'We take the wagon,' said Cortez. 'Five of us. We can kill the guards and take their rifles. Then we shoot the two up on the hill and ride the wagon out. By the time the men on the watchtowers see where we're going, we'll be out of range.'

'Where are we going?' asked Oveda. 'The only way out leads back to the rail station.'

'We split up,' said Cortez. 'Before we reach the station, we all spread into the hills. You stick with me. They'll never find us up there.'

Oveda nodded his agreement: even possible death was better than the cockroaches and the beatings.

'Leave it to me,' said the Villista. 'I'll give you the word.'

It came three days later.

Oveda was lined up behind Cortez in the long queue for food. The two cook-guards were doling out a thin mixture of beans and soup while the three regular men stood laughing at the prisoners with their Winchesters cradled in their arms. The other two were squatted down higher up the rocks, passing a cheroot between them.

'Now!' shouted Cortez.

He lifted his arm as he said it, exposing the rock hidden in his fist for the moment it took to swing his arm back and hurl the stone at the nearest guard.

The flint took the man between the eyes as he began to look up at the shouting. It burst his skin, sending him staggering back against the wagon with his hands fumbling numb for the rifle. Cortez was on him before he could lift the gun, ramming a knee into the *federale*'s groin so that the man doubled over. Cortez grabbed hold of the Winchester either side of the guard's grip, and lifted it up. The guard kept hold, so that his arms were stretched above his head. Cortez forced the gun up and back as his right knee lifted against the *federale*'s chin. Then he brought his arms down, slamming the length of the rifle against the base of the man's skull as his knee continued to lift the chin.

The guard's neck broke like a rotten twig. His eyes gaped wide. Then closed. And a thin spurt of blood erupted from his mouth.

Oveda gaped in amazement as the *federales* died.

He saw a prisoner he had never spoken to before slam a piece of sharpened flint into a guard's stomach. Saw the prisoner twist the stone knife; and saw the thick blood spurt out from the grey uniform as the flint lifted clear to hammer against the face.

Another man hurled his slop into the face of a guard and then swung the tin plate like a discus against the eyes before fastening both hands on the *federale*'s throat and beginning to beat the head against the ground.

A bullet ruptured splinters from the wagon, and Cortez shoved a rifle into Oveda's hands.

'Come on!' he yelled. 'Let's go!'

Oveda stared curiously at the rifle. He had never held one before. Then he saw one of the cooks stumbling clear of the wagon with blood running down his face and a Colt's Thunderer in his hand. Oveda didn't know what kind of gun it was, just that it was dangerous. And pointing at Cortez's back.

He pointed the Winchester and squeezed the trigger.

The cook went backwards with most of his pot belly spraying out behind him. There was a long, thick spurt of blood that seemed to suck him in as it gouted from his back, and then a spill of entrails from the front of his stomach.

Oveda laughed: the eruption of death had caught him up into its wild chaos. He levered the rifle again, watching the cook's face distance itself from reality as his bullet sharded teeth into the throat and nostrils. As the back of the man's skull came clear on a solid fountain of blood and sticky, grey brain matter.

He turned, seeing a man in the sweaty-stained cotton tunic of a prisoner struggling with a *federale.*

The *federale* was trying to draw the pistol on his belt. His face was thick with blood where the stone the prisoner was pounding against his arm had broken his nose and blinded one eye.

Oveda pressed the Winchester against the *federale*'s side and squeezed the trigger.

It felt good to see the blood come out from the other side of the hated uniform. It was some kind of an answer; he couldn't say just how, or why, but it felt very good. Even better when the guard toppled over into the puddles of his own blood.

'Quick!' yelled Cortez. '*Vamanos!*'

Oveda climbed into the wagon alongside the Villista. Another man climbed onto the left-side of the seat, and he was aware of more clambering into the back.

Cortez whipped up the ungainly mules, urging them to a gallop.

Oveda looked round, and saw six men in the rear of the vehicle. They were hurling pots out and laughing at the prisoners remaining inside the confines of the canyon. He clutched the Winchester across his chest and hoped they wouldn't need to kill any more.

They hit the open road that went by the fort at full gallop. It was packed firm out of Santa Granada onto both sides of the canyon, and the mules were plunging in the traces with Cortez slashing a whip over their hindquarters and yelling like an Indian.

His yelling got counterpointed by the stutter of the machine guns on the watchtowers of Santa Granada.

They sounded dull, a curiously disinterested sound that was more like the clatter of knitting needles than any imminent announcement of death.

Until the canvas of the wagon stitched open and the screams lifted like flames from the back.

Then they became real as men pitched over with heavy calibre slugs stitching their bodies apart, filling the wagon with blood.

The guns traversed forwards, and Oveda saw a multiple spray of dust lift from the ground. Like fountains of sand that the mules ran into and went down in, with their legs and chests and hindquarters spraying a secondary fountaining that tinged the yellow dust dancing of the bullets with spurts of crimson.

Ramon Cortez lifted clear of the wagon with his left arm reaching out forwards, where the machine gun had severed the elbow so that his hand was still fastened on the reins as the mules went down and separated his limb from his body.

He screamed again as he hit the ground, his body bouncing with the stump of his arm spraying blood all over the sand.

Oveda felt his seat lost as the wagon swung sideways.

He pitched clear with more energy than he thought he had, and hit the ground with a solid thump as the wagon piled into the dead mules and rolled over Cortez's body with an ugly, squelching sound.

He shook his head, wondering why it hurt so much, and stood up.

He was yards clear of the spilled wagon, down in a gulley that looked to run westwards. The Winchester had gotten lost somewhere down the line, so he forgot about it and began to run.

He was out close to the end of the gulley when the *federales* showed.

They were on horseback, holding Mannlichers.

He looked at them, his face filthy with blood and dirt, staring at them the same way a frightened rabbit might look at the hunter.

And they came down as fast as they could, the rifles swinging in practised unison against his skull.

When he next awoke he was inside the courtyard of Santa Granada.

There were seven bodies spread on the sand before him, and when he got his eyes open enough to focus on the whole vista, he saw that there were four more.

They were alive: lashed to the posts driven upright from the sand of the central area of the prison. They were tied to the posts with thin twine that bound their wrists, behind the posts, like the cord holding their heads upright.

He felt himself picked up, and heard Colonel Alcaza say,

'This is a stupid thing. No one escapes from Santa Granada. Not from my prison. This will prove it to you. All of these men tried to escape. And see what happens to them!'

He turned to face the chubby commander and was suddenly aware that the whole prison was turned out.

Suddenly aware that he was held up by two guards.

A spectator to a failed escape.

There were faces staring at him.

Accusing: Juan Oveda.

The intellectual.

The failure.

The one who got saved.

He closed his hidden eyes and went on staring – fascinated – at the men tied to the poles.

'They need not have died,' shouted Alcaza. 'If men like him,' – he pointed at Oveda – 'did not give them ideas. Now see where those ideas take them.'

Alcaza raised his arm.

Twelve rifles lifted to the firing position.

He dropped his arm, and the same twelve barked shots.

The men lashed to the posts jerked under the fire, heads and legs twitching against the constraints of the ropes.

Blood showed on their chests, and they slumped silently forwards against their bonds.

Oveda bent over to vomit.

'That upsets you?' asked Alcaza. 'Why?'

'That was murder,' groaned Oveda. 'You needn't have killed them.'

The commander of the Santa Granada prison laughed and said, 'You're lucky. It could have been you.'

Oveda started to ask why, but a rifle butt slammed against his head and he went down into a swirling pool of darkness that bore as much relation to life as a dream.

When he woke, he was back inside a cell.

He could tell it wasn't his first one by the difference of the light.

The first had had some faint glow coming in from under the door. This one had no light at all. And the walls were damper. When he touched them, they felt to be running with water. The floor, too, felt wet.

Inside the darkness – like a child afraid of the terrors hidden in the shadows – he checked his cell.

He kept his eyes closed, frightened of what he might see as he fumbled around the parameters of his new prison. It was six paces in either direction, the only break in the uniform configuration the window built through the door. The door itself was set flush against the stone of the walls, the wood covered with the same wash of viscid fungus that covered the walls.

The floor was bare, except for a single couch with rawhide straps forming a basis for a mattress; which he didn't have.

He had nothing, except the darkness and the damp.

He settled on the empty bed-frame and went to sleep.

It would have been good to escape from Santa Granada.

Could have been.

Had it been possible.

But it hadn't – wasn't.

So he went to sleep.

# *Chapter Eleven*

León was built at the apex of a high, uplands valley. It was contained on both sides by the tall ridges emanating in a vee-shape on a southwesterly line, down which ran a narrow, fast-flowing river. West of the Gringos' position there was the slender line of the railroad, the tracks glinting in the afternoon sun. Beside the metal highway there was the width of the main trail curving into the city before trail and tracks alike got lost amongst the buildings.

Onslow swung his binoculars slowly from left to right, then back, noticing that the rails were still in place, the bridge spanning the river still intact. There was an artillery piece dug in at the northern extension of the bridge, and machine gun posts were sandbagged in place either side of the rails, commanding the approaches of the tracks and the trail alike. Closer to the city there were more *federale* positions, the grey uniforms joined by the paler tunics of the regular army. He moved the binoculars, tracing the line of the rails into the town. There was an area of sidings and engine sheds that was thick with uniforms, and inside the confines of the city the streets were busy with soldiers. He scanned onwards, picking out the *federale* barracks set in back of the main plaza; the massive bulk of the church with its huge bells set atop the tower. There were three hotels and more cantinas, a variety of stores, and then private houses and warehouses set back from the centre on a network of roads and alleyways. Towards the edges of the valley, the city petered out into a spread of miserable-looking adobe shacks and scrubby smallholdings. Higher up the flanks, and along the line of the depression, there were rich-looking fields, dotted with storage sheds.

The city looked busy and prosperous. And nervous.

'It's crawling with troops.' Onslow passed the glasses to Strong. 'They must be expecting Villa.'

'One thing's sure.' Strong handed the binoculars on. 'We go in there, we're dead.'

'Christ!' McCloud lowered the binoculars. 'You ain't kidding.'

Jamie Durham just whistled.

'You said you could help us.' Onslow turned to Raza. 'How you reckon to do that?'

The silver-haired man shrugged and pointed to the head of the valley. 'You see the tracks there? That's the line out to Santa Granada. Prisoners are brought in to the main depot and then transferred to the secondary line. The tracks run through the pass into the hills. The gradient is very steep, and if there's a particularly heavy load they put a second locomotive on the tail. When the train reaches the bluff, it halts. They take the second locomotive off and send it back down to León. There's a little water halt at the top, then the line runs on to the prison station.'

'And then the prisoners get loaded into wagons,' grunted Onslow. 'And it's a five mile run to the prison. That's the hard part: getting close enough to get inside. That and finding Oveda.'

'That's how I can help you,' said Raza, lighting a cigar. 'The commander of Santa Granada is a man called Alcaza. He's a friend of my friend. That way, I can find out where Oveda is held.'

'That's only part of it,' said Onslow slowly. 'Knowing where he is ain't getting him out.'

'But if you had *el coronel* Alcaza?' suggested Raza. 'What then?'

An idea began to form in Onslow's mind. It was pretty wild, but accepting this crazy mission in the first place had been pretty wild. He nodded, his eyes thoughtful.

'You ain't gonna trust him?' McCloud broke the silence. 'Jesus! Onslow, the man's just said he's joining someone working with the *federales.*'

'In troubled times it is as well to have as many friends as possible.' Raza drew on his cigar, unperturbed. 'And after the attentions *capitán* Montes paid my daughter, I have little love for his kind.'

'I don't trust him,' snarled McCloud. 'I say we kill him before he gets a chance to sell us out.'

Onslow turned to look at the Southerner. He remembered the time McCloud had done the same thing, and for a moment he felt pure hate for the man. Then he reminded himself that McCloud seemed to have changed: had become a useful member of the team. Though whether that was simply because McCloud had nowhere else to go – like most of them – or because of a genuine feeling of kinship, he couldn't tell.

'Shut up, Yates,' he murmured. 'This could work.'

He turned to stare at Raza.

'Yates has a point. We don't know you're not taking us into a trap. Now we've got you here, you could give us away.'

Raza shrugged. 'And you could denounce me as a Villista.'

Onslow nodded. 'Maybe. But that wouldn't count much against capturing us: we need some kind of insurance.'

'Keep his money,' urged McCloud. 'Keep the gold.'

'No.' Onslow shook his head. 'That don't solve it. We need his help. I don't think gold buys that.'

'Hold the *señorita.*' Strong smiled apologetically at the girl. 'Until we've got Oveda.'

Carmen started to protest, but her father waved her to silence.

'All right. Keep Carmen.' He turned to Onslow. 'But you must give me your word she will not be harmed.'

'You got it,' said the tall man, tugging at his moustache. 'Now listen.'

Carmen Raza watched her father head down the slope with Onslow and Strong. She was frightened to see them go, not only because her father was leaving, but also because the tall *gringo* was leaving with the big Negro: somehow she felt these two held the others together. Held them in line.

Maybe not so much the strange young man with the leather mask on his face, because he seemed rather pleasant, but the other one. The one they called Yates.

The one with the dirty eyes.

She sat down, watching the figures recede into the distance as Jamie got a fire started and began to brew coffee, and McCloud opened a bottle of tequila.

Onslow and Strong were riding the mules. They both wore *serapes* draped over their clothes, and Onslow had replaced his stetson with a wide-brimmed Mexican sombrero. Strong went bare-headed; but who looked twice at a black servant?

They rode behind Raza, like servants.

The Mexican led the way to the outskirts of León, then turned off into side streets that circled round the city to the east side. They crossed the rail tracks and moved south, curving round clear of the main part until they were in the suburbs beyond and climbing the far slope towards a white-painted hacienda with a high wall running all around.

Raza halted at the gate and reached over to haul on a rope. A bell clashed, and a *mestizo* almost as dark as Jonas Strong opened the gate.

They rode on up a gravelled pathway to a colonnade of arches overhung with hibiscus and oleander.

Raza dismounted as a very tall, very thin man, with a neat beard and no hair on his head, came out to greet them.

'Luis Bedoya,' said Raza. 'This is Cade Onslow and Jonas Strong. They want to rescue someone from Santa Granada.'

Bedoya frowned, and Onslow's hand tightened on the grip

of the Colt Automatic. From the corner of his eye he saw Strong's *serape* shift slightly as the Negro took hold of the cut-down Remington.

'Come in,' said Bedoya. 'I don't like Villistas, but I like Santa Granada even less.'

They went inside a spacious house that seemed all tiled floors and white-washed walls that were covered with paintings. Bedoya took them through to a study where the whitewash was hidden behind oak panels and shelves heavy with books.

He produced a decanter of American whiskey and filled four glasses.

'Tell me,' he said, 'how you think I can help.'

Raza explained.

'Suppose it fails?' asked Bedoya. 'What happens to me then?'

'That's a chance,' admitted Onslow. 'I guess they'd hang you.'

'Or you'll shoot me,' said the Mexican. 'That's not much of a chance.'

'Villa will be here soon.' Onslow sipped his whiskey and looked hard at the bald man. 'He won't be stopped now. He's got his whole army on the trains, and León is the next stop. Obregon's coming down the west coast, and Zapata's moving in from the south. Before very long, Huerta is gonna fall. Anyone who helps in that direction will be a friend of the new government.'

'Of bandits,' said Bedoya. 'If Villa takes power.'

Onslow shrugged. 'That's not my worry. Getting inside Santa Granada is. And anyone who stops that ain't going to be friends with Pancho. On the other hand, if someone helped us, then Pancho would be more favourably disposed.'

He stopped speaking and drank his whiskey, letting the implicit threat sink in.

Bedoya and Raza were of a kind. They had no political convictions, nor much social conscience. Their commitment was to the making of money, for which purpose they were prepared to accept any kind of government – so long as it allowed them to go on doing what they did best. Raza had sensed the wind of change and decided to sell up, to take his chances abroad until things calmed down and he could come home again. Bedoya had chosen to stay. But staying meant facing Villa and his bandit army, and there was little chance of the government forces winning. Even if they fought Villa to a standstill at León, there was still Zapata closing in on Mexico City from the south, and Obregon leading the Carranzistas in the west. So Bedoya wasn't left with much chance at all: he could prove his loyalty to Villa and hope the bandit-revolutionary would look kindly on him, or he could refuse to help and anticipate the full weight of Villa's wrath.

'All right,' he said. 'I'll help you. What do I do?'

Onslow grinned and accepted a fresh glass of whiskey.

'You think we'll be moving soon?' asked Jamie Durham. 'I'm getting twitchy.'

'I don't know.' McCloud shrugged. 'Depends on Onslow. Him an' his Mex friends.'

'I hope it's soon.' The Kid scratched his arm. 'I can't hold out much longer.'

'We got some action right now.' McCloud looked at Carmen Raza. 'Right here.'

'Leave it,' said Jamie. 'We got trusted to guard her.'

McCloud went on grinning. 'I wasn't thinking of nothing else.'

The girl tugged her jacket closer about her body, trying to hide her figure inside the confines of the loose-fitting coat. She wished she hadn't taken off her hat to let her hair fall free, but it was too late to do anything about that now. She also wished that the fair-haired man would stop looking at her the way he was. Especially when he kept on sucking the tequila.

After a while McCloud moved away from the tree he was leaning on.

'There's nothing happening,' he said. 'They must've got in safe. So we got a day at least. Maybe more.'

'Shit!' Jamie shivered despite the heat. 'I can't hold out that long, Yates.'

'So do what you gotta,' said McCloud. 'I'll watch things.'

'All right.' Jamie went inside the tent. 'Thanks.'

He rolled up his sleeve and opened the oilskin pouch. He wanted to sterilize the needle, but felt curiously embarrassed to do it in front of the girl. So he settled for dipping the needle in tequila before tightening the strap around his arm and clenching his fist to bulge the veins out. He winced as the point snaked inside a vein, the withdrawn plunger sucking out bright red blood. It paled as he drew up the morphine, the colourless liquid weakening the stark crimson of the original intake.

Then he clenched his fist again and sank the point into a vein.

Depressed the plunger, watching the level go down as he sighed.

He set the hypodermic back in its case and tugged the thong clear of his arm. Then he put everything back in the kit and fastened the oilskin closed before stretching on his bedroll as he waited for the peace to come.

Outside, Carmen Raza stared nervously at Yates McCloud. The Southerner had been drinking steadily since mid-afternoon, and now that the shadows were growing longer he tossed the empty bottle aside and stared back.

'You're pretty.' His words were only slightly slurred. 'Real pretty.'

The girl smiled nervously. 'Thank you.'

'Yeah, real pretty.' McCloud fetched a fresh bottle from his saddlebags. 'Prettiest woman I seen in weeks. No! In months. You want a drink?'

'No.' Carmen shook her head. 'We must get food ready.'

'Food?' McCloud took a long swallow and giggled. 'Food's work for wimmen. That an' other things.'

'I'll get it ready,' she murmured. 'The food.'

'Be better if you got somethin' else ready.' McCloud poured more liquor down his throat. 'Beats eatin' any time.'

'I don't understand you.' As she said it, she knew she was lying: just trying to stall him. 'What do you mean?'

'This,' said McCloud.

And slumped to the ground beside her with one arm, his left, dropping around her shoulders.

Carmen tried to escape, but his left hand dug deep against her arm, forcing her down and round as his right trapped her chin and turned her face towards him. He kissed her, and when she pursed her lips tight closed he fastened his thumb and forefinger against her jaw and sprung her mouth open.

He tasted of liquor and tobacco, and as he kissed her, he dropped his right hand inside her jacket, clutching at her breasts.

She pulled away, simultaneously afraid of what he obviously planned to do, and at the same time of risking offending him.

'What's the matter?' The way McCloud said it, it came out as: *'Wash the marrer?'*

She shook her head, wanting to spit. Wondering if she could fight him off.

'Come on.' McCloud shifted his weight so that he had her pinned to the ground. 'It's been a long time.'

As he said it, he stroked her hair, his hand trailing down over the long, thick curls until it reached again inside her coat. Abruptly, he lifted up, dragging the jacket down over her shoulders so that her arms were held until he dragged the garment free. When she tried to hit him, he caught her wrists and forced them behind her back. Then he transferred his grip so that both her arms were held inside the spread fingers of his left hand. His right went down the front of her blouse, ripping the buttons loose.

The shirt fell from her body, exposing sweetly cusped breasts, the dark-ringed nipples erect with fear. McCloud bent his head, fastening his mouth over one nipple. His left hand still held her arms entrapped, and he had a leg over her thighs, holding them down. His right hand fumbled at her pants, unfastening the belt and ripping the buttons loose.

She began to scream, but his mouth blocked off the cry, and she felt her pants torn from her legs and realized that she was naked, save for her boots and the remnants of her shirt.

A finger probed between her legs and she tried to close her thighs.

But McCloud was too strong. He pinned one leg across hers and used his knee to force the other wide: the finger went on probing. Then he stopped, still holding her pinned down, and reached to unfasten his flies.

She felt the cool weight of his penis against her crotch as he lowered himself onto her and tried to close her legs again. McCloud swung his right hand against her face.

Once.

Twice.

A third time.

The slaps stung her cheeks and numbed her mind. Bright lights danced over her eyes as her hands reached up to claw his face. He knocked them away, sending them sliding down his body.

'It's inevitable,' he gasped. 'So enjoy it.'

One hand touched his gunbelt, and she recognized from somewhere inside her panic that she could save herself. She stopped struggling, letting her hands wander to the butt of the pistol.

She had it halfway clear of the holster before McCloud realized what she was doing. And then he snatched the Lightning from her hand and hit her hard in the mouth. The gun scudded over the grass as her head went back with blood coming from her nose. She groaned, and McCloud laughed, pinning both her hands against the ground as he lifted back to thrust into her.

And then something hit his head. Hard. At the base of the skull. Sending lights spinning crazily across his eyes as a numb, dumbing shock ran down his back.

Then there was a blow that seemed to evaporate the air from his lungs and he was rolling over, sucking wind as his belly exploded into fire.

He came up on his knees, gasping for breath as he stared at Jamie Durham.

The Kid was staggering, eyes glazed and feet unsteady. But the Colt's Thunderer he held pointed on McCloud was rock-steady, angled at the Southerner's belly.

'Leave her,' said Jamie Durham. 'Don't mess with her, Yates, else I kill you.'

'Me?' McCloud got up on his feet. 'Why?'

'She ain't no whore.' Jamie had trouble enunciating the words. 'Not some cantina lady.'

'So?' asked McCloud. 'So what?'

'So we got trusted to look after her,' said the Kid. 'The major told us. We promised him that. Him an' Raza. Her, too.'

'Shit!' McCloud snarled. 'She's one more Mex bitch. We lost that money her old man was hauling, so why not enjoy her?'

'I'll kill you if you try,' said Jamie. 'I swear it, Yates.'

'You'll be out in a while,' said McCloud. 'Gone off on that goddam dream of yours. What you gonna do then?'

'Give her the gun,' said the Kid. 'And if you try anything, I'll kill you when I wake up.'

'If you do,' sneered McCloud. 'If you do wake up.'

Jamie shrugged. 'I'll chance that, Yates.'

He toed the girl's coat over the grass and motioned for her to put it on. Then, still holding the Colt on McCloud, he backed inside the tent. Carmen Raza went with him.

'Listen,' he said, stretching out on the bedroll, 'if Yates tries anything, shoot him.'

Carmen nodded as she took the gun, and Jamie closed his eyes and went away into the dream.

It was a good dream this time . . . .

. . . It had Carmen Raza in it.

She was standing by the creek, wearing a white dress. And he touched her; held her. And she laughed with joy, and stepped away from him, opening the dress. And then she was naked, calling him to come on and enjoy her.

And then they were standing in a church, still both naked, as the priest announced the blessing and great fluttering streams of white and pink confetti fell across his eyes.

And he woke up, reaching for his water bottle as he felt the fur in his throat, then changing his direction to fumble for the gun on his belt.

'It's all right,' said a familar voice. 'Come on, Jamie, it's all right.'

He opened his eyes and looked at Cade Onslow.

'Where's Yates?' he asked. 'He here?'

'Outside,' said Onslow. 'He's got a sore head and a sorer gut, but he's all right.'

Jamie sat up. Carmen had gone, and when he asked Onslow where, the tall man said:

'We found her in here. Watching you like a mother wolf. Yates told us most of what happened. She was guarding you.'

'That's nice,' murmured Jamie. 'That's real nice.'

When he got outside he felt embarrassed again: Carmen had seen his addiction, and somehow that wasn't like the others seeing it. He washed his face and dragged a razor over his cheeks. Then he drank some coffee and went over to the girl.

'You all right?' he asked. 'Nothing happened?'

'No.' She smiled at him. 'Nothing at all.'

He looked over to where Yates McCloud was sipping

coffee, one hand pressed to his belly, and started towards the man. Onslow stopped him.

'Leave it, Kid. Best I handle this.'

Jamie nodded, and hunkered down beside the girl. He watched Onslow walk over to where McCloud was leaning back against a tree and halt, looking down at the Southerner.

'I thought I could trust you, Yates.' A cold bitterness belied the mild tone. 'I thought you learned your lesson.'

McCloud shrugged and went on drinking coffee. Onslow sighed, then lashed out with his right foot, kicking the mug from McCloud's hand.

'Jesus Christ! What you do that for?' McCloud came up on his feet, wincing as he straightened his stomach. 'What's wrong with you?'

'What's wrong with you?' asked Onslow, low and cold; angry. 'Can't you hold off the bottle? Can't you hold off women?'

McCloud licked his lips, his eyes shifting anywhere but to Onslow's face. 'I got a bit drunk, that's all. I thought to have me some fun with the Mex girl.'

'I gave my word she'd be all right,' said Onslow. 'I promised.'

'Maybe you should have asked me first,' said McCloud. 'I never made no promise.'

'I thought we had that sorted out.' As Onslow got madder, his voice got colder. 'Don't you ever learn?'

'Guess not.' McCloud began to grin. 'I guess I'm just a good ole Southern boy, who knows where to take his pleasure.'

Onslow's hand came round open. The palm landed hard over McCloud's cheek, the impact leaving a pale area on the tan. It snapped McCloud's head to the side, the movement halted and reversed by the back-hand swing that snapped his mouth closed. Both cheeks went pale, then a deep flush suffused the skin with beetroot red, and one hand dropped to the butt of the Colt's Lightning.

Onslow's Automatic came out faster. His thumb snapped the safety catch clear of the casing and his hand shut tight on the secondary, butt-mounted safety. The ugly black bore pointed like an accusing eye at McCloud's face. There was an infinite moment when Onslow thought the Southerner would go on drawing the Colt and force him to squeeze the trigger. It was tempting: he almost wished it would happen.

But then McCloud eased his fingers clear of the Lightning's butt and let the pistol drop back into the holster. He smiled.

'Didn't know it would upset you so much, *major*.' The accent on the title was back in his voice. 'I shoulda remembered how you feel about Mex women.'

Onslow's thumb flicked up to snatch the hammer back, and McCloud's smile went away as he looked into the cold eyes that promised him death.

In that long instant he knew that he had said the wrong thing. The one thing, perhaps, that would make Onslow kill him. Out of hand: like a mad dog. Onslow seldom referred to his Mexican wife, but McCloud knew she was the reason the ex-Army man was fighting Huerta. Knew that government forces had killed Linda Onslow soon after their marriage, thus prompting Onslow to side with the Villistas. Knew that Onslow still cherished the memory.

And knew that he was very close to death.

'No!' Jonas Strong's shout rang across the hillside. 'Don't, Cade! He ain't worth it.'

Very slowly, the hammer of the Colt went down, then Onslow lowered the muzzle. He holstered the big pistol, still staring at McCloud.

'The last time, Yates.' His voice was dull, picking each word with a flat, deadly coldness. 'The next time, I kill you.'

'Yeah.' McCloud felt his face go red with embarrassment. 'I understand.'

'You better.' Onslow turned away. 'You surely better.'

'So what we doing?' McCloud tried to save face. 'What's our next move.'

'We're going into León,' said Onslow. 'Raza's set up a meeting with the boss man of Santa Granada.'

'Christ! You're crazy.' McCloud shook his head. 'I ain't going down there.'

'Yes you are,' said Onslow. '*El jefe*'s bringing four *Colorados* with him, so I need four men.'

'Go to hell!' snapped McCloud.

'We're maybe all on our way,' said Onslow. 'Get mounted for the ride.'

# *Chapter Twelve*

They entered the city one hour after sun's set, skirting round the peripheral buildings to approach the southern slope of the valley wall on a slanting angle.

There was a gate at the rear of the Bedoya hacienda where a servant waited with a carefully-dimmed lantern. He opened the gate and led the way through the grounds to the rear of the house. There was a stable, where they left the horses and the mules, and then the same servant took them inside the main building.

Bedoya and Raza were waiting for them.

There was a meal ready in one of the rooms at the back of the house, and Bedoya had set bottles of whiskey on the table. They sat down to eat, discussing the strategy Onslow had worked out.

It was, in theory, simple: Santa Granada was commanded by *coronel* Felipe Alcaza. Bedoya had made it his business to make friends with the *federale* because that was the best way to get his farm produce bought for the prison. He now supplied all the food, in addition to stocking the *federale* barracks in town.

He was trusted.

So he knew that an elite squad of *Colorados* was due to arrive in León the next day. Alcaza had told him they were coming in to beef up the defences against Pancho Villa, led by a *commandante* Montes. Bedoya – on instructions from his good friend Alvaro Raza – had invited *coronel* Alcaza to bring *commandante* Montes and his three most senior officers to dinner.

Tomorrow.

At seven o'clock.

'They are coming with a fresh trainload of prisoners,' he explained. 'The train will be left in the sidings throughout the night, and move on to the prison in the morning. The officers have separate quarters to the men, and as it is a new command for Montes, not many people know him.'

'How's that help us?' asked McCloud. 'Jonas ain't gonna pass for no Mex officer, an' Jamie ain't exactly inconspicuous.'

'The water halt,' said Raza. 'Remember?'

'Yeah.' Onslow took up the plan. 'The train sounds like a big one, so it'll most likely stop at the crest. Bedoya says that Alcaza often gets drunk down here an' catches up later, so there's no reason why his new friends shouldn't do the same.

'So, we wait up here and take them. We keep Alcaza alive to get us inside the prison. We're dressed in *Colorado* uniforms and we're with the commander. No one's gonna look too close. We board the train at the halt and ride it through to the station. Me and Yates are best likely to pass for Mexicans, so we ride up front.'

'That's one hell of a long shot,' said McCloud. 'How do we get out?'

'Jamie sets some bombs,' said Onslow. 'And we take Alcaza out with us. It's the best chance we got.'

'I best get to work then,' said the Kid. 'I'll need to get things ready.'

Onslow nodded, and he went out to the stable, where his explosives were neatly stacked inside an empty stall.

He opened the bags and began to arrange the deadly materials with the same care he applied to his drug kit. Villa had given him exactly what he asked for: gelignite sticks and dynamite; a selection of fuses and cap; phosphorus flares, and the delicate percussion caps that would explode if a man trod on one. Even softly.

He spread a tarpaulin over the floor and set the stuff out in neat lines, working under the light of three kerosene lanterns. He prepared a series of standard blasting charges that needed only the fuse lit to set them off, and a series of trickier bombs that could be spread around for the unwary to tread on. In addition, he made up some grenades and some flare bombs, both of which could be thrown.

He was finishing when Carmen Raza came into the stable.

'Don't come no nearer!' His voice was harsh with anxiety. 'It's dangerous.'

She stopped, staring at the array of cylinders and round, black bombs.

'What are you doing?'

'Getting ready.' Jamie began to pack the explosives with straw, preparatory to stowing them back inside the saddle-bags. 'Don't worry about it.'

'I wanted to thank you,' she said. 'For what you did.'

'All right.' The Kid finished loading the explosives. 'You thanked me. Thanks.'

He stood up, dusting his hands carefully before washing them: gelignite was tricky to work with.

The girl stayed watching him. She had changed from her mannish clothes into a dress of green silk that was a little too big for her slender frame. It hung away at the shoulders and breasts so that she kept reaching up to lift a fold into place.

'Why do you wear that mask?' she asked. 'What happened to you?'

'I got hurt,' he said. 'My face got blown away.'

'Show me.'

'No!'

He backed away from her, one hand reaching instinctively to check the leather patch that covered his scars. She smiled and came forwards.

'I'm not afraid of what you look like. Please. Show me.'

Jamie Durham felt a wall block his escape and reached out to take the girl's hands before they could touch his mask. The next thing he knew, he was holding her on the straw of an empty stall and her oversized dress was coming clear of her breasts as his shirt slid from his body. He felt her reach down to his pants and rolled clear, unbuckling his gunbelt – remembering enough to lay it clear where he could reach it fast.

She giggled and asked him why he kept a knife inside his belt.

'Protection,' he grinned. 'Against assault.'

Then – just like the dream – they were naked. Her body was lithe and brown, long legs fading into a dark thatch of pubic hair that matched the colour of the tresses spread over the straw. Her breasts were firm, the nipples only slightly paler than her hair, erect and eager as his mouth touched them. He felt the moistness between her legs and moved on top of her; anxious, now.

'Wait. Wait.' She laughed, stroking his body, her hands moving upwards. 'I want to see your face. All of it.'

'No,' he said. 'For Chrissakes! No!'

But her hands were already on the fastenings of the mask and before he could stop her, she had pulled it free.

It hung in her right hand: a small piece of leather.

And her eyes closed and her mouth opened in a scream that Jamie blocked with one spread hand.

Then her eyes opened again and he felt a shudder run through her body as she stared at the ugly purple scar tissue that covered the left side of his face. Her mouth moved under his retaining grip, and her eyes got wider still as she stared at his deformity.

He felt the excitement leave her body.

Felt his own erection dissipate.

And rolled clear.

'I didn't know,' she said. 'I didn't know how ugly you are.'

He didn't reply. Just rolled over and buried his face in the hay as she got dressed.

'I'm sorry,' she said. 'I didn't know.'

Jamie went on crying until he heard the stable door slam

shut. Then he pulled his clothes back on and went over to his saddlebags.

He pulled out his needles, and without bothering to sterilize anything, pumped a fresh load of morphine into his arm.

Then he went back onto the straw and waited for peace to come.

. . . It came fast, but not easy.

He saw the stream again . . . the willows and the aspens running alongside the creek . . . Saw a girl – she might have been Mary Reilley or Carmen Raza – it was hard to tell.

She opened her dress so that it fell lazily about her legs, and beckoned him on. But each time he tried to touch her, she was gone. And then she was resting on the bank, legs spread wide, an enticing smile on her face. But when he reached for her, he was face down in the stream, with fishes blowing bubbles into his eyes and laughing as they darted inside his mouth.

He screamed, and the sound became a spurt of crimson that gouted from his mouth and nostrils to curl in the air above like the smoke of a campfire. He heard a horse snort, and the snorting became a wavery line of yellow bubbles that broke over his head and threatened to suffocate him until a mule brayed, producing a thick line of liquid blue that wrapped him in darkness and blotted out everything else.

'Christ! What made him do this?' Onslow looked at his companions. 'You know why?'

'He fixed the bombs,' said Strong. 'Looks like they're ready, at least.'

'We need Jamie to set them,' said Onslow. 'Goddamitt! He's the only one knows how.'

'He'll be all right come morning.' McCloud sipped whiskey, suddenly aware that he was needed again: in a position of control. 'Let's get him up to his room. I can handle him after that.'

'Why?' Onslow repeated. 'Why'd he do it?'

'I saw the Mex . . . The Mexican *lady,*' said McCloud. 'Going out of the house. I think she came here.'

'How'd that upset him?' asked Onslow. 'That much?'

McCloud reached down to the floor of the stable and picked up the mask.

'She saw his face, maybe?' He went over to where Jamie was asleep and set the leather patch inside the Kid's right hand. 'He wouldn't like that. Maybe she didn't, either.'

'He best be fit tomorrow,' said Onslow. 'Else we're all blown.'

'He'll be all right,' answered McCloud. 'Come morning, he'll be up and running.'

They lifted Jamie Durham from the straw and carried him to the room Bedoya had given him. It was on the first floor of the house, with a big bed at the centre that Jamie sank into like a sleeping child. McCloud fixed the mask over the Kid's face before leaving him.

'He'll feel happier,' he said, 'if he wakes up with that to comfort him.'

Morning brought shame to Jamie Durham.

He felt guilty for no reason.

Felt dirty for no reason.

He felt he had every reason to feel both.

He washed and shaved, staring at his sad, scarred face, thinking about Carmen Raza.

Then he took a bath and dressed in his last clean shirt. His pants were still dirty, but at least they were pressed by Bedoya's servants. He fastened them, then buckled his gunbelt around his waist.

Tucked the switchblade into its familiar position.

He checked the load and went down to breakfast.

A servant ushered him through the house, and he realized that he was late.

*Fuck that,* he thought, *They still need me. I'm still the only one knows how to use explosives. I'm the only one can do that. So they can't work without me.*

He touched the mask covering the left side of his face and went into the room.

Luis Bedoya was sitting up at the head of the table with Alvaro Raza and Carmen to his right and left. Then there was Cade Onslow facing Yates McCloud, and Jonas Strong looking at an empty chair.

Carmen looked down at her plate as he came in, but Onslow grinned and said:

'How you feel?'

And Strong lifted his fork to point it at the empty seat.

And even Yates McCloud shifted the chair out from the table and said, 'Come eat. It's pretty good.'

So he sat down. And it was good: he hadn't realized how hungry he was.

He forked the eggs into his mouth and chewed the tacos like a man starving. He drank five cups of coffee, and two second helpings of eggs; then began to feel human again.

He even watched Carmen excuse herself from the table – still without looking at him – and quit the room.

'It happens tonight,' said Onslow. 'We all ready?'

'No,' said Jamie. 'I got the explosives ready, but I don't know what to do tonight.'

'They come in for dinner,' said Onslow. 'Alcaza's a little, fat man. He'll be sitting next to *señor* Bedoya, where *señor* Raza is now. We keep him alive. Kill the others.'

'Finc,' said Jamie. 'Easy. Silent or noisy?'

'Silent,' said Onslow. 'No point to making noise.'

'No,' said the Kid. 'No point at all. It disturbs too many dreams.'

'Tonight,' repeated Onslow pointedly. 'Be ready. All of you.'

'Don't worry,' murmured Jamie. 'I'll be ready. I'll be ready and I'll enjoy it.'

# Chapter Thirteen

It was strange, the dual effect impending action had on him.

It had always excited him, producing a kind of elation that was simultaneously heady with anticipation and tinged with fear. Back in the Army, when his unit was readying for a move against Mexican bandits or one of the few remaining bands of hostile Apache, he had felt that same sensation. Afterwards, after the mine had exploded in his face, it had changed. The fear had grown stronger.

Not fear of death. That – especially now, with his face scarred – seemed unimportant. A thing to be avoided if possible, but not a thing to dwell on, or care much about. No: the fear had to do with fouling up. With making a mistake. He got scared of feeling his addiction hit him in the middle of a mission, of getting the shakes when his hands needed to be rock steady when a trembling finger could slip a primer and detonate a parcel of explosives. Or groaning as some guard went by.

It was a fear of letting down the others. Of proving himself unable to meet Onslow's exacting standards of professionalism.

And the only way to avoid the fear was to pump more of the drug into his arm, balancing the dose so that he felt confident it would see him through. Then he was all right: his hands remained steady and he felt in control. He enjoyed the action when it came, exulting in his deadly skills like a child with expensive toys.

The trouble now was that Carmen Raza had thrown him off-balance. He had planned to fix up at dawn, allowing one full day for the morphine to take him away and bring him back, calm and ready. But now he was worried that he had used the stuff too early, that the effects would wear off sometime during the assault on Santa Granada. And now it was too late to shoot a second load – that would leave him too weak to handle the attack.

He slumped against the bole of a luxuriant cherry tree, smelling the perfume of the blossoms as the sun struck his face and the enclosed garden got bright as his thoughts were dark.

A shadow fell across him and he looked up at Yates McCloud.

'The girl give you a bad time?' The Southerner appeared to have forgotten their fight. 'That the problem?'

'How'd you know?' Jamie went on staring at nothing as McCloud hunkered down beside him.

'Ain't hard to guess.' McCloud lit a cheroot and began to blow smoke. 'I saw her heading for the stable.'

Jamie nodded without speaking.

McCloud said: 'She saw your face. So then she pulled a fast turn on you. Right?'

'Something like that,' Jamie acknowledged. 'Damn' bitch.'

'They're mostly the same.' McCloud shrugged. 'Lead a man on, then turn off if he don't live up to expectations. That why you used the needle?'

Again Jamie nodded.

'And now you're worrying about it wearing off.' McCloud reached inside his coat to fetch out a small parcel wrapped in greasy paper. 'This might help.'

Jamie took the package, unfolding the paper to reveal a small fruit, not much larger than a cherry.

'Some kind of peyote,' said McCloud. 'It's real mild, but it should help you through.'

Without waiting for an answer, he got to his feet and sauntered back towards the house. Jamie stayed seated, staring at the little cactus. It was one of the constantly surprising things about Yates McCloud: he always knew where to find things. And – usually when least expected – he came on friendly.

Jamie put the fruit in his mouth and began to chew.

Onslow's plan was a mixture of simplicity, opportunism, and audacity. The fortuitous meeting with Raza had given him a chance to get inside Santa Granada and locate Juan Oveda without risking a forced break-in, and he had taken full advantage of the opportunity. It remained a dangerous manoeuvre, but – given the chance – it seemed the best way of bringing off the escape.

The way he had it mapped out, they would capture Alcaza and kill the four *Colorados* that night. Taking the uniforms of the dead men, they would board the train with Alcaza as cover. Get inside the prison and use the *coronel* to locate Oveda. With sufficient explosives going off, they should have a reasonable chance to get out again – still with Alcaza as a shield.

Bedoya would provide horses for a getaway, and the impending arrival of Villa and his bandit army should tie-up most of the León garrison enough that they could reach the hills and hide out until the Villistas came in. Or go back to León.

Bedoya was a potential weak link, but Onslow thought the Mexican too scared of Villista repercussions to risk betraying them. And after the *Colorados* had died, he would be sacrificing his own neck if he went to the *federales*.

It was simple.

And very dangerous.

Onslow stretched on the soft bed, running the moves through his mind. Hoping.

Hoping nothing prevented Alcaza and the others from turning up at the hacienda.

Hoping they came alone.

Hoping Alcaza would be too scared to betray them.

Hoping they could get out again.

Hoping . . . .

Jonas Strong checked over the horses. Bedoya's servants had rubbed down his own mount and the Kid's, and both animals appeared in good condition, ready to run again without flagging. The *hacendado* had given Onslow and McCloud two fresh animals, both in prime condition. One was a rangy bay gelding, all chest and legs; the other was a big black with the same look of power about it.

Strong went over the beasts like a breeder at an auction. He checked the teeth and the cruppers, the legs and the hooves. He bent the knees and lifted the tails. They were sound.

Then he checked over his guns, sitting inside the stable with the warm, friendly smell of horseflesh all around him.

He didn't think at all about Santa Granada.

Yates McCloud left Jamie Durham and wandered back inside the house. There was no one inside the study, so he poured himself a big whiskey and drank it slowly as he stared out the window at the motionless figure of the Kid.

He felt sorry for the poor little bastard.

Christ! To get that mess made of your face, that was really something. Enough to throw any man off kilter. No wonder he'd got hurt when that Mex bitch backed off of a tumble in the hay.

The thought reminded him of Carmen, and that brought a hardness to his pants. He wondered where she was now – he'd noticed she was staying away from them all since last night.

Then he thought about the little *mestizo* girl he had seen in the kitchen. She had smiled when he flirted with her, and there was a distinct feeling that she was available.

McCloud poured himself a second whiskey and went to find her.

She was just finishing her chores. Looking the worse for having spent most of the time since before dawn scrubbing dishes and preparing food. Her hair was tugged back behind a sweatband, and her hands looked rough. But her mouth was large, wide-lipped, and her figure was young and strong.

Thirty minutes later McCloud was discovering just how strong as the sun filtered through the shutters of his room and the girl held him gripped between her thighs.

'This is crazy,' said Bedoya. 'All of it.'

'Mexico is crazy,' replied Raza. 'This war is crazy.'

'But we could be shot,' said Bedoya, 'if the *federales* find out.'

'We could be shot anyway,' grinned Raza. 'By anyone.'

'But keeping these *mercenarios* here,' Bedoya protested. 'Letting them kill *Colorados* here.'

'Villa will be here soon.' Raza poured them both more tequila. 'It will be very good for you if he knows you helped these men.'

'And if he doesn't come?' Bedoya questioned. 'And Huerta stays in control?'

'Hagh!' Raza waved a dismissive gesture. 'Huerta is finished. That's why I'm getting out. Anyone who stays will have to get on with the *peons*. With the Villistas and the Zapatistas. Carranza is better, but he'll be influenced by the others.'

'Huerta is fighting hard,' said Bedoya. 'You could be wrong.'

'Listen,' said Raza, 'there's a war in Europe now. Germany is too busy fighting to help Huerta any more. England is fighting Germany, so she won't help us. And America has finally chosen to side with the rebels. You know why? Because the rebels are winning, *amigo*. Because Zapata has the South cut off, and Villa rules half the North. Carranza has his "government" up there in Nogales, and his man – Obregon – is coming down the Pacific coast. Huerta is finished, so a sensible man switches his bets.'

'To the winning side,' murmured Bedoya. 'I hope.'

'These Gringos are good,' said Raza. 'Good tools. And you can trust Onslow: he keeps his word.'

'I don't have much choice, anyway,' said Bedoya. 'Do I?'

'Not really,' agreed Raza. 'Except to use them to help you.'

The day began to fade into evening. The sun went down behind the distant mountains and the valley got filled with a warm, golden light. A breeze started up out of the hills, rustling the voluminous flowers of the cherry tree, murmuring through the hibiscus and the oleanders. The bees drifted back to their hives and the scratching of the cicadas got louder.

Jamie Durham woke up.

He shivered, then smiled from under his mask: he felt good. All the fear was gone, replaced by the keen anticipation of early action. He stood up, stretching as he went over to the stable.

Inside, he checked his explosives and then his guns. He spent thirty minutes honing the edges and point of the switchblade to lethal sharpness. And then, whistling, he went into the house.

'All right,' Onslow said. 'You wait in here.'

He gestured round the large room. There was a table at the centre with ten chairs flanked against the sides and heads. It was already set with silver cutlery and decanters of cut glass. There was a staircase leading up to the first floor and four doors opening off the room. One opened onto the vestibule, a second into Bedoya's study; the third went to the kitchens, and the fourth to a ladies' withdrawing room.

'Jamie, you're best with a knife.' Onslow pointed at the balcony overlooking the room. 'Can you hit a man from up there? Clean and fast?'

Jamie climbed the stairs and hung over the balcony, calculating distances and angles.

'Yeah,' he said. 'I can.'

'Two?' asked Onslow. 'Can you handle two?'

'If the second knife's balanced right,' nodded the Kid. 'Sure. But why?'

'This has to be fast and silent,' said Onslow. 'Way I see it, Jonas stays back in the kitchen to take one of the *Colorados.* Yates is in the little room over there. He comes out behind while I do the same from the other side. We need to kill them fast. And without making a mess of the uniforms. Then we have to cover Alcaza.

'If you can take two out with knives, that'd make it all a whole lot easier.'

'Fine,' said Jamie. 'Seat two either side of this end of the table an' you got it.'

Onslow looked at Bedoya, who nodded.

'All right,' he said. 'I will put Alcaza at the head. So Montes and his second-in-command will sit either side of him. I will take the other end, and for God's sake please be careful.'

Jamie chuckled. 'Don't worry, *señor.* I'll throw straight.'

'That's it,' said Onslow. 'That's how we'll do it. Go find the other knife, Jamie.'

Thc Kid went into the kitchen and appropriated a wide-bladed skinning knife. It wasn't built exactly as he would have liked, but it was the best he could find: the hilt was honest wood, riveted through the extension of the blade, which was honed sharp on both sides and needle-tipped. He took it out to the stable and spent some time raising the edges to even brighter sharpness, then spent thirty minutes practising throwing it, until he was confident of the balance.

After that, he grabbed a quick meal with Onslow and the others and watched Raza and Carmen disappear into their rooms before taking up position on the balcony.

'Remember,' called Onslow. 'Fast and silent. No noise; no mess. Start on my signal.'

'Sure,' said Jamie, feeling the confidence flood back into his mind, knowing he could do it. 'Don't worry.'

# *Chapter Fourteen*

'Welcome,' said Luis Bedoya. 'It is good to see you again.'

'Thank you,' said the plump commander of Santa Granada. 'It is good to find a friend in these troubled times. Permit me to present my colleagues.'

'I am honoured,' said Bedoya. 'But first, a drink. *Si?*'

'*Si,*' said Alcaza. 'You still have that American whiskey?'

'Enough.' Bedoya filled six glasses. Up to the tops. 'For tonight, at least.'

'*Gracias.*' Alcaza lifted his glass. '*La victoria!*'

The others followed the toast and Alcaza made the introductions:

'*Commandante* Raul Montes. *Capitán* Moros. *Capitán* Angeles. And *teniente* Herramo.'

'Gentlemen,' said Bedoya, 'I am pleased to see you. I feel sure you will settle many problems here in León.'

'You worry about the Villistas?' asked Montes. 'Why?'

'They seem to get closer every day,' Bedoya shrugged. 'One never knows where they will be next.'

'Where they belong,' said Montes. 'Fertilizing the ground after we stop them here.'

'You are very confident,' said Bedoya, unpleasantly aware of the ears listening to his speech. 'It's reassuring.'

'Listen,' said Alcaza. 'The *commandante* has a full troop of *Colorados* with him. This business with the prisoners is just an easy way to get him here. His men are now in the town, supporting the regular forces. I should have told you before, but,' he shrugged, 'you know what military regulations are like.'

'So the *commandante* is expected back tonight?' asked Bedoya, feeling his face get pale. 'At his command?'

'Don't look so disappointed,' laughed Alcaza. 'He'll stay long enough to enjoy your dinner. And some of that excellent wine you serve.'

'I shall be honoured,' said Montes. 'I am not expected back until the morning, at the earliest.'

Bedoya filled the glasses again, and after a while they sat down to eat.

There was a soup – *gazpacho* – that was accompanied by a cold, dry white wine from the Loire valley in France. Then hare, cooked in red wine and herbs, with a claret to wash it down. After that, steaks seeded with peppercorns and bathed in a sauce that was thick and rich and pungent. Bedoya served imported French beaujolais with that.

The dessert was pineapple, soaked in German kirsch. Then coffee and brandy and cheeses.

Alcaza and the four *Colorados* ate very well, and drank better. And by the time Bedoya was passing round the cigars and refilling the brandy glasses, Onslow decided it was time.

He came out of the side door with the Colt's Automatic in his hand.

He yelled: 'Now!'

And as he pressed the Colt against Moros' temple, Jonas Strong came out from the kitchen and slung the length of his hefty black arm under Alcaza's chin, hiking the head back and up with the sawed-off Remington sticking hard into the gaping mouth.

Simultaneously, there was a blur of movement from the balcony. Jamie Durham lifted to his feet and brought the switchblade he had clutched in his right hand up and over, sending it down in a flash of lamplight to imbed against the base of Montes' throat.

The newly-appointed *commandante* was just starting to turn in Onslow's direction, so the whole left side of his neck was exposed, the veins drawn tight by the movement.

Jamie's knife went in hard and deep. It cut the jugular vein and grated against the upper linkages of the spine. Montes started back in his chair, his hands reaching towards the blade. Then they fell loose as he began to choke on the emptying of his life.

A thin trickle of blood ran down his neck between his collar and his shirt, then a secondary flow started from his nostrils and mouth as he slumped forwards, bleeding into the remains of his meal.

The second knife landed in *capitán* Angeles' right eye as he turned towards his commanding officer. It sliced through the eyeball like a blade cutting butter, the point driving on into the brain before the wide edges grated on the cut sockets of the drained eye and brought the knife to a stop. It was still propelled with sufficient force that Angeles' head was knocked back, the shock of the pain numbing his mind long enough that Onslow could reach him before he screamed.

Moros was already dead. The surprise of the Colt against his head had stilled his voice. And Onslow had wasted no time: he had lifted the gun and driven the butt against the *Colorado*'s temple at the same time as he dragged the man back over his chair and then slammed the pistol hard down against the nub of the adam's apple, smashing the knot of cartilage into Moros' throat. The *Colorado*, half-blinded by the blow to the temple, had begun to choke. And Onslow had lifted the Colt another time and slammed the metal edging of the grips down against the man's skull, impacting the upper casing of bone into the brain so that Moros' own protection killed him.

Onslow lifted the Colt and brought it down hard against the hilt of the knife sticking out from Angeles' eye.

The blow drove the blade deeper in, cutting a swathe of torn flesh from both sides of the eye, and forcing the knife into the brain. Angeles' body jerked clear of the chair, carrying Onslow with it as rictus motion threatened to spill the table over. Onslow let go the Colt and went down with the man, reaching over to grasp the hilt of the knife and wriggle it deeper into his brain.

Angeles died fast after that, kicking against the table as his dying brain gave up on his limbs and let them fall supine into the long sleep of death.

And across the bloody room, Yates McCloud was choking *teniente* Herramo.

The Southerner was using a length of cord that would normally be used to hang meat. He had fashioned a knot at the centre of the length, and more at either end, to allow his hands a grip. The cord was wrapped tight into Herramo's neck, wound round once with the knot pressed tight against the adam's apple. McCloud had his knees jammed against the lieutenant's back, and both hands high out of reach as the choking soldier fought to loosen the cords binding him to death.

His face went pale. Then red. Then got suffused with purple as the interior blood vessels burst and his eyes bulged and his tongue stuck out, all black and swollen. Then there was a low, slow gargling sound from deep inside his body and a thin spread of urine flowed over Bedoya's floor as he died.

McCloud dropped the cord and spun the body away from the urine.

Bedoya stared round in horrified amazement as the bodies were lifted from the blood and stripped of their clothes.

Alcaza, too, stared in shock, not daring to speak for fear of triggering the shotgun still planted in his mouth.

'Don't worry,' said Jonas Strong. 'You just do what we say, and you live. You spoil it, an' you die. *Comprende?*'

Alcaza might have nodded, but for the scattergun.

'Godammit!' Yates McCloud tugged uncomfortably at the dead man's pants. 'Why'd the bastard hafta to do that?'

'Guess you just scared the piss out of him.' Jamie fastened the upright collar of a captain's uniform about his neck. 'How'd I look?'

'*Muy bueno.*' The Southerner parodied a salute. 'Real military.'

It was only in part a joke: the uniform had an effect on the Kid that seemed to make him brace his shoulders back and stand straighter. The cap served to draw attention away from the leather patch covering half his face, hiding most of his fair hair, so that he suddenly assumed the appearance of a hard-bitten *Colorado*.

The same was not true of McCloud. The lieutenant's uniform fit him well enough, but he seemed uneasy in military garb, as if his instinctive dislike of discipline extended even to the disguise. His dandyish good looks were lost under the grey of the tunic, the jacket slightly too large for his frame, the stained trousers lending a faintly ridiculous air.

'All right, quit admiring yourselves.' Onslow turned towards Alcaza. 'We got things to do.'

The short, plump officer sat nervously at the head of the table, Strong's shotgun touching the nape of his neck. His face was pale, the forehead sheened with sweat and his teeth nibbling at his lower lip. His hands were spread on the table before him, the fingers trembling slightly against the blood-stained cloth. 'You understand what you have to do?' Onslow stared down at the smaller man. 'You got it right?'

'*Si! Seguro.*' Alcaza nodded, repeating Onslow's instructions like a child anxious to please its teacher. 'I get you on the train. You are officers from Divisional Headquarters sent to inspect the prison. I get you inside the walls and show you where Oveda is held. Then I get you out again. Then . . . .'

His voice tailed off as a cold smile crossed Onslow's face.

'Then – maybe – we let you live,' said the American. 'If you do everything just like you were told.'

'You can't!' Bedoya spoke for the first time since the slaughter. 'He'll have me shot.'

'Not with Pancho due to arrive any day now,' answered

Onslow, cynically. 'He can just take off his uniform and tell how he helped the rebel prisoner to escape.'

'No!' Bedoya reached for the brandy. 'You can't take the chance. It could be my life.'

'I don't kill unarmed prisoners.' Onslow's voice got cold. 'Not even men like this.'

Without waiting for a reply he motioned Alcaza to his feet and led the way from the room. The *hacendado* watched him go, followed by the others. Then he slumped in a chair and reached for the decanter again. He was downing his third fast brandy when Alvaro Raza came down the stairs.

'*Jesus Cristo!*' The silver-haired man crossed himself. 'It's like a slaughter house. We must get rid of the bodies.'

'*Madre de Dios!*' Bedoya shook his head. 'What have I gotten myself into?'

'A war,' said Raza, bluntly. 'A very bloody war.'

Outside, the four Gringos mounted the dead officers' horses. Onslow, wearing the major's uniform, sided Alcaza. Jonas Strong and Jamie Durham followed, with Yates McCloud bringing up the rear. Each man had replaced the *Colorados'* guns with their own weapons. Onslow had the Mauser strapped outside his tunic, the shoulder rig complementing the cross-straps of Montes' Sam Browne, while Jonas Strong carried the cut-down Remington slung at his right side. The Kid's horse was bulky with packages of explosives.

Off to the east, where the head of the valley was located, the sky was just starting to get light. The night chill was fading, the transition from coolness to warmth lifting a mist from the ground that swathed them in grey vapour. León was very quiet, settled into that transitional period between night and dawn that is neither one thing, or the other. The period when men dream of past pleasures or past sins; or of those to come. Somewhere up ahead a cock crowed, the stridency bringing an answering challenge from the south, and then a third from the west. And then, abruptly, the sky seemed to open, a long, thin finger of light cutting through the clouds so that for a moment the whole of the eastern skyline was brilliant. And then, as suddenly as it had come, the light dimmed, the clouds rolling back, though now tainted with a reddish gold along their undersides, and a single, far-off peel of thunder ripped the air.

They rode in silence, holding to a steady trot that took them through the outskirts of the city to the farmland beyond. A quarter mile out from the last of the houses, the trail looped to the north, picking up the single line of railroad tracks that ran alongside the river. The stream was more narrow there, cut down between walls of water-washed stone five feet, or more, deep, the river gushing noisily down towards the city. The double line of the rails shone with a silvery glitter in the gloom, marking their route better than the dark trail that was flanked by stands of low-lying timber and thick spreads of sweet-scented shrubbery.

After a while, the trail curved away from the tracks and began to climb upwards. It followed a series of wide curves that took them steadily higher as it wound towards the pass. They came out onto a small plateau a hundred feet or so below the summit, and saw the sun come out for sure through the clouds. The pass got outlined in brilliant light, the walls gleaming gold as the day began, the radiance throwing the blunt shapes of the buildings flanking the water halt into stark perspective.

Behind them, a locomotive howled a single, long call.

They rode on up to the halt.

Four sleepy-eyed *federales* under an unshaven sergeant manned the stop, along with two employees of the railroad. They seemed unsurprised to see Alcaza, and went about their business without looking too closely at the others. The Gringos stayed back in the shadows beneath the water tank until the train pulled in, then moved towards the car Alcaza indicated.

The train was hauled by a big four-wheel locomotive with a cowcatcher out front and two flags waving either side of the smokestack. There was a timber wagon immediately behind, and then a flatbed with Lewis guns mounted behind sandbags on both sides. After that, there was a small passenger car, and then three long cattle trailers. There were arms waving from between the slatted sides of the trailers, and voices asking for water. Behind the last wagon there was a brake-van, with two more Lewis guns bolted to the safety rail.

The convoy soughed to a stop with the locomotive under the water tank. The engineer swung out the hose and dropped it neatly into the boiler as *federales* clambered down from the passenger car and began to fill canteens for the prisoners. Onslow linked his left arm through Alcaza's right, and Jonas Strong tucked the scattergun under the *coronel*'s armpit as he faked support on the left.

'Remember you're drunk,' whispered Onslow. 'You don't have time for no one.'

Whether from fear, or a talent for acting, Alcaza gave an excellent impersonation. He tottered towards the passenger car with his head flopping from side-to-side and his legs shaky. Onslow climbed the steps and halted at the door. There was a *federale* lieutenant just inside the long-aisled carriage, sucking on a pipe with his feet up on the opposite seat.

'*Por favor*,' Onslow rasped. 'The colonel needs help.'

'*Lo siento!*' The man came up on his feet with the pipe disappearing into his tunic. 'I didn't know.'

He saw the markings of a *commandante* of the *Colorados* on the uniform and snapped off a neat salute.

Onslow smiled: one military man to another.

'Check the rear,' he said. 'The colonel is *uno poco borracho*. He doesn't want to be disturbed.'

'*Claro! Claro!*' The *teniente* moved down the car. 'I'll keep the men to the rear.'

'*Gracias*,' smiled Onslow. '*Muy gracias*.'

'*De nada*,' replied the lieutenant, thinking about promotion. 'It's nothing.'

Onslow turned back to face Alcaza as Strong pushed him up. The little fat colonel was shaking all over now, and the two Americans needed to support him as they headed for the front of the car.

Onslow took the most forward seats, the ones facing the door onto the observation platform. He settled into the right-hand, outer position, with Alcaza jammed up between him and Strong. Yates McCloud and Jamie Durham took the seat across the aisle, with the Kid's bags resting between them. When the guards got back on board, it was noticeable that they left a wide space – maybe three full rows – between themselves and the *Colorados* escorting *coronel* Alcaza back to Santa Granada.

There was a screech of escaping steam from the locomotive, followed by the shrill squeal of the whistle, and then the whole caboose lurched forwards with a shuffling motion that threatened to shake everyone from their seats.

'Christ!' grunted McCloud. 'We could get killed by this goddam driver.'

'*Collarse la boca,*' snapped Onslow. 'Shut up! We're Mexican, remember?'

McCloud nodded. '*Seguro. Lo siento.*'

'If I gave the word now,' said Alcaza, seeming to emerge from his fear-induced trance. 'You would all be killed.'

'You wouldn't be around to watch it,' murmured Strong. 'Not with your head plastered to the roof.'

He smiled as he said it, crossing his arms so that the shotgun angled up at the Mexican's face. Alcaza swallowed hard and forced an expression midway between a smile and a contortion across his lips.

'There's not a damn' thing you can do, *coronel,*' said Onslow. 'Except go along with us.' He paused. 'Unless you really want to die.'

The locomotive shuddered into a slightly higher gear, easing up the slope like a tired *peon* hauling a cart to market. Alcaza slumped back against the seat, closing his eyes as though he hoped he was dreaming and when he woke up the nightmare would be gone.

It didn't go. The locomotive went on dragging the cars up the rise to the apex of the pass. High walls of rock, dotted with scrubby pines, lifted up on both sides. The *federales* stayed quiet at the rear of the car and the train went on chugging over the back of the ridge. The day got bright as they went through the pass and the slope inclined in the opposite direction. The locomotive ran freer here, the brakeman in the hindward car locking his wheels in place as they went down the slope that opened into the wide valley containing Santa Granada.

The rock spread back on either side like an opening fan, covered with timber at the beginning, but then parching out into slopes of bare shale and naked stone as the valley got wider. It was hot, the floor of the enormous spread of land becoming sand as they progressed deeper into the long cleft. There was little vegetation, not even many cactus plants, to break up the depressing view of empty ground. The sun got hot on the windows, and Onslow opened the forward door, letting in a breeze. It was as sticky as the wind washing from a Chinese laundry, but at least it imparted movement to the air along with the smoke coming from the stack of the locomotive.

They rode in sweaty silence for two more hours and then the whistle screamed again and the brakes locked in to slide the train to a stop along the length of a godforsaken platform that had nothing on it but a single adobe shack and a whole lot of *federale* uniforms.

There were two rows of iron-caged wagons drawn up alongside the station, and a single six-seater buckboard with a canopy over the top. Onslow kept Alcaza inside the train until all the prisoners were loaded into the prison cages, then went out of the train with Jonas Strong close behind the fat commander of Santa Granada. Two captains and three lieutenants snapped off neat salutes as they escorted the *coronel* to his waiting buckboard.

When the dust had cleared, Onslow nudged Alcaza, and the Mexican ordered the driver forwards. The man nodded without speaking and took the four-horse team out at a fast trot a hundred yards wide of the slower-moving column.

The valley leading up to Santa Granada was wide and flat. Bottomed in sand, it shone yellow in the afternoon light. A blinding, searing yellow that scorched the eyes and coated faces with a near-solid layer of grit that lifted from under the hooves of the horses and the wheels of the buckboard to blow back and up against the travellers. Off to the sides, walls of hard stone lifted steadily higher, as though they rode into the rocky hands of some inconceivable giant waiting to scoop them up and crush them. There was no foliage here; no timber or brush, not even cactus plants: just the spread of emptiness that shone eye-watering under the sun.

And then, like an ugly monolith built to depress men even further, they saw the walls of Santa Granada.

It was square and flat and ugly. Sheer-sided walls lifted up near as high as a three-storey house; featureless. Blank. Except for the towers built up on the corners and the two matching posts either side of the gate.

Each tower held a machine gun. It was hard to define them through the heat haze, but Onslow thought they were Maxims from the belts swinging from the breech blocks and the men crouched beside the gunners. There were, he noticed, one on each tower: a total of six.

With the two flanking the gate combining with the two on the western-facing walls to cover the entire approach area to the prison.

Or the escape area.

He turned to Jamie: 'Take out those machine guns, Kid. They have to go, if we want to get out.'

Jamie nodded, not speaking.

'And tell the driver that he's coming with us.' Onslow turned back to face Alcaza. 'Tell him that if he wants to stay alive, he does exactly what we tell him. Just like you.'

Alcaza nodded, sweating some more, and spoke fast with the man in the seat.

The man nodded and spat. He angled the expectoration so that it flew back and plastered stickily against Alcaza's face. And he grinned as he did it.

And the Gringos came up to Santa Granada and went inside the forbidding walls, listening to the gates swing shut behind them like a coffin lid closing.

# *Chapter Fifteen*

The driver took the wagon across a parade ground-sized square of sand with a flagpole at the centre and, off to the left, four six-foot stakes. The sand was darker around the stakes. A flat block of two-storey adobe occupied the centre of the compound, the windows barred and the single door manned by two guards carrying rifles. There were more buildings set in tight against the exterior walls; barracks, stables, a cook-house. Behind the central block there was a row of smaller buildings, where the driver brought the buckboard to a halt.

'My quarters.' Alcaza answered Onslow's frown. 'They're private.'

'All right.' Onslow climbed down. 'Yates, get that wagon put away, then bring the driver back here.'

McCloud nodded and settled into the seat beside the driver.

'You married?' he asked pleasantly. 'Got kids?'

The man nodded. '*Seguro. Tres.*'

'You want to see them again,' smiled the Southerner, 'you keep your mouth closed. I'm a *Colorado* come to look around this shit pile. You say anything else – you're wife's gonna be looking for a black dress.'

The driver nodded again. 'I will not say a word, *señor*. Except maybe to cheer when you kill that fat pig Alcaza.'

'Cheer soft,' grunted McCloud. 'An' walk cautious.'

'Will you take me with you when you go?' asked the driver. 'I never wanted to be here. I want to join the Villistas.'

'Ain't that the way?' McCloud shrugged. 'Maybe.'

They crossed the sand to a corral and the driver handed

the team to an ostler. McCloud did his best to look fierce and forbidding, like an elite officer. The ostler stared at the red band around his cap and took his eyes away from the scowl on the Southerner's face. McCloud nudged the driver and they started back on foot for the colonel's quarters.

Inside, the room was cool and quiet. There was a table at the centre with chairs spaced around it, and a desk against one wall. A bookcase held military manuals and tequila, and the only other item of furniture was a deep, leather armchair. There was one other room, containing a bed and a dressing table.

Both rooms were empty.

'Where's Oveda?' Onslow took the Colt from the flapped holster, tugging back the hammer and snapping the safety into place before dropping the gun back inside the leather. 'You got a map?'

Alcaza nodded, pointing at the desk.

Jonas Strong went over and opened it, rummaging through the papers until he came up with a scale plan of the prison.

Juan Oveda was held in a cell underground, two levels down. The way Onslow read the plan, there was just one entrance to the prison block, with a contained stairway going down to the first subterranean level, then a second to the next. Both were contained by metal doors, and there were guards on each level; more above.

'How many men?' asked Onslow. 'Guards?'

'One hundred prisoners below,' said Alcaza. 'Three hundred on top. There are twenty guards at each level, and thirty in the main hall.'

'That's one helluva lot, major,' murmured Jonas Strong. 'That many don't give us much chance.'

'No,' said Onslow. 'They don't.'

It was a time for fast thinking.

For flexible thinking.

And Onslow was good at that. The original simplicity of

his attack plan was getting clouded by the suddenness of events. Ideally, he would have spent time scouting Santa Granada, finding out exactly how the prison was run. Not going in before he knew just how many guards there were and how they operated. But the opportunity of taking Alcaza had over-ridden that cautious approach in favour of gaining easy entry to Santa Granada.

Now he needed to adjust his plans.

'All right,' he said, reaching a fast decision. 'We play it different.'

He broke off as the door opened and Yates McCloud pushed the driver through.

'He wants to come with us,' said the Southerner. 'He says he never wanted to join up, but now he wants to fight with Villa. Thinks the old *coronel* there is a real pig.'

'Tie him up,' said Onslow.

McCloud grinned and snatched his Colt from the holster. The rubber-gripped butt of the Lightning slammed against the side of the driver's neck and he slumped down into unconsciousness. McCloud used a torn-up sheet to bind and gag the man.

'Jamie,' said Onslow, 'can you fix a bomb to go off here about thirty minutes after we leave? A big one?'

'Fix it for dead on,' nodded the Kid. 'How big?'

'Enough that this building gets blown apart,' said Onslow. 'With a lotta fire.'

'You got it.' Jamie began to open his bags. 'Biggest bang you ever saw.'

'Good.' Onslow turned to Alcaza. 'Now: I want you to order Oveda brought up here. You tell your people you want a wagon laid on because the *Colorados* are taking him back to León, and you're going with them.'

'*Si,*' nodded Alcaza, terrified. '*Si. Claro.*'

'That's why you kept the driver here,' added Onslow. 'You understand?'

Alcaza nodded some more, sweat running fast down his pudgy face.

'Trains,' said Strong. 'What about trains?'

Alcaza smiled through his sweat. 'There will not be another train for three days.'

'There has to be a way he contacts them,' said McCloud. 'I saw telegraph wires as we came in.'

Onslow took the Colt Automatic from his holster. His thumb snapped the safety catch down from the hammer, leaving only the pressure of his hand off of firing the .45 pistol as he touched the muzzle to Alcaza's head.

'Well? You want to tell us?'

'Land lines.' The Mexican gulped, slobbering his words out as the heavy gun fetched fresh sweat from his forehead. 'I can call one up.'

'Good,' said Onslow. 'You do that. Now!'

He stood back as the shorter man rose to his feet. Jonas Strong went over to the door, opening it and sliding behind its cover with his shotgun pointed at Alcaza. The action made a loud noise sliding back, and the dumpy commander of Santa Granada mopped his face.

He stepped onto the porch with Onslow's words echoing inside his mind.

*Remember! You speak one wrong word and you're dead!*

'Bring Juan Oveda up here,' Alcaza ordered the sergeant who appeared on the porch. 'Then bring a wagon over. Don't worry about a driver: I have one already.'

A long thirty minutes later a man was thrust through the door. Alcaza dismissed the guards under the context of a *Colorado* interrogation and closed the entrance.

The man was totally bald, except for a sparse beard that was slimed with vomit and thick with insects. He wore a cotton tunic that might once have been white, but was now grey with sweat and dirt. His face was pockmarked with open sores, and his bare feet were covered with bite marks and congealed blood.

His eyes were vacant, not looking at anything.

'Oveda?' Onslow asked. 'Are you Juan Oveda?'

'*Si, jefe! Que quieren?*'

He shuffled into a ragged facsimile of the attention position as he said it.

'We come to take you out,' said Onslow. 'We're going to set you free.'

'*Si, jefe! Gracias, jefe.*'

'Jesus!' said McCloud. 'Did we come in here to rescue that?'

'Shut up!' snapped Onslow. 'Oveda! do you understand me?'

'*Si, jefe.*'

'Oveda!' Onslow stepped closer. 'You *are* Juan Oveda?'

'*Si, jefe.*'

'He's Oveda,' said Alcaza. 'I promise you that.'

'You better be right,' said Onslow. 'Christ! You better be dead right.'

'Wagon's here,' called Strong. 'Fresh horses an' two men.'

'Right.' Onslow turned to Alcaza. 'Tell them to get lost. We got our own driver.'

Alcaza nodded and went out onto the porch. Onslow and Strong crouched behind the windows as the Mexican dismissed the handlers and Yates McCloud brought the original driver out from the bedroom.

Jamie Durham ignored them as he laced both rooms with explosives, concentrating on his work. He left a series of dynamite sticks around two sides of the office and the bedroom, all linked to a single fuse. He planted an incendiary bomb inside the desk and another under the bed. Then he set a trip wire across the door, connected to a grenade and an incendiary, so that anyone trying to enter would trigger off a secondary explosion.

'We ready to go?' he asked. 'Now?'

'Yeah.' Onslow nodded. 'Let's make it fast.'

Jamie grinned and struck a match, touching the flame to the tip of the long fuse.

'We got thirty minutes less one,' he said. 'Before the biggest bang of them all.'

They went out to the buckboard and climbed into their places. The driver whooped the horses up and they skirted round the spread of buildings towards the gate of the fortress.

No one tried to stop them. The gates just opened to let them through, as the soldiers atop the towers saluted Alcaza.

They covered a quarter mile of open ground and then Jamie Durham called for the wagon to slow down as he dropped from the back and seeded the ground with mines. Then he climbed back in and they rode hard for the rail station.

They were a long way from Santa Granada when the explosives went off. They heard a dull thudding sound, like faraway cannon, and saw a thick plume of smoke lift from above the prison.

Inside, it was worse.

The explosion devastated most of the adobe buildings housing the officers. There were nine of them – Alcaza's second-in-command, four captains, and four lieutenants – eating inside the thin walls of the adobes. The dynamite Jamie had left exploded the walls outwards, spreading a fragmenting pattern of flying stone and heated plaster outwards across the sun-baked sand. At the same time, the interior walls collapsed, blasting through into the adjoining quarters so that the entire row of buildings collapsed. The incendiaries washed flame over the ruins, adding fire to the damage and the problems of the men inside the prison.

The entire senior corps of Santa Granada was destroyed in one devastating blow, leaving only a junior lieutenant in any kind of command.

He sent a rider after *coronel* Alcaza, but when the rider was a quarter mile from the prison he disappeared inside a puff of smoke.

*Teniente* Barraez ordered a second man out, watching him

through binoculars. He saw the man head fast towards the body of the first rider, then saw him lift into the air as his horse bucked upwards with a flash of fire that was swiftly covered by a cloud of smoke. When it cleared, he saw that the horse was stretched on its side with most of its stomach hanging out, and the rider was clutching at his eyes as his legs bled his life away.

The lieutenant ran for the telephone, knowing that something was horribly wrong.

The line was dead.

'It's cut,' said McCloud. 'Like them: cut off.'

'Good,' said Onslow. 'Now all we need is the train. Let's go.'

They rode on to the station.

The same lazy-eyed *federales* were on duty, talking amongst themselves as a small shunt engine puffed wearily up the slope with a single car behind. The day was getting dark, and the smokestack of the locomotive sent showers of bright sparks upwards against the night sky.

Onslow turned to Jamie Durham: 'Best they don't have a chance to follow, Kid.'

Jamie nodded, understanding. He felt good: pitched up high on a peak of excitement. He moved into the shadows and began to seed the rails with bombs. He enjoyed what he was doing: improvising against the unexpected. He set a series of bombs under the tracks, linking each one with a fuse that was connected to a detonator. Each detonator was linked to a second fuse that, in turn, was connected to another detonator. It was a complicated pattern, but the way he had it worked out, the train would spark the first caps as it pulled into the station. He had allowed for a thirty minute turn around, during which time the first fuses would burn into the second set of caps, and thirty minutes after that, the whole railhead would get torn up.

He hoped they were clear by then.

If not, they were in deep trouble.

The engine came on up the slope, the solitary lamp mounted ahead of the catcher throwing a pale gleam of light through the growing dusk.

They heard it coming before the light shone round the bend in the rails. It was a tired, lonesome sound. Empty of hope, but full of despair; like a *peon*'s widow dragging herself home from the fields.

And then the light shone bright and the engine chugged to a halt beneath the overhang of the sign that read: *Santa Granada.*

The *federale* sergeant saluted as they climbed on board and shouted an order at the engine driver.

The locomotive sighed.

Shuddered.

And went into reverse gear.

It began to clatter down the slope, wheezing as it hit the higher grades, then running smooth as it took the descent into León.

Juan Oveda slumped back against the hard wooden seat of the single coach. He couldn't understand exactly what was happening.

Another trick?

Were these men real *Colorados*?

Or real Villistas?

It was difficult to tell: they seemed to act with the same harsh assumption of authority the *Colorados* displayed. Yet they had taken him out of Santa Granada.

But to where?

León, yes.

But why?

Up the ridge a series of explosions went off. For maybe ten minutes there were lights playing across the darkening sky.

Bright lights that erupted in flaring brilliance through the dark before smoke clouded out their illumination. Like fireworks seen from far off. Like carefully placed explosives detonating the way an expert would place them.

They lit the ridge like the fourth of July. Or the feast of San Juaquin.

And for the first time in months, Oveda laughed.

Back at the station sergeant Emiliano Torro got picked up into the air with fragments of broken rail shattering through his body. His men were beside him, so they, too, got caught by the explosions. Only two were killed – Torro and a trooper called Vissamez – the others were wounded, or blinded. One never spoke again because the hot metal of the exploded rails burned out his tongue.

The railhead was destroyed: a three hundred yards length of track was torn up into crazy patterns that would take weeks to fix back in place.

Santa Granada was cut off.

The locomotive tugged into the buffers of the León yards.

'Let's move,' said Onslow. 'Fast!'

They came down with Alcaza and the driver herded to the middle, and got as far as the exit gate of the yards before a *federale* lieutenant said, 'Villa is attacking. He's got field pieces. We can't last much longer.'

'*La viva*,' said Onslow. 'You never know what life brings.'

The man shrugged, frightened of arguing with a *Colorado*.

And Onslow led the way through the streets of León.

They got back to Bedoya's hacienda and let the driver go free. He ran into the streets, stripping off his uniform as he raced down the slope.

The Gringos climbed into their own clothes.

'And him?' asked McCloud, pointing at Alcaza. 'What about him?'

Onslow looked at the chubby Mexican as the dull thud of artillery shells shook the walls of the house.

'Let him go,' he said. 'No point to keeping him here. Not any more.'

Alcaza ran into the street. He headed towards the rail depot, hoping to find escape to the south.

He was unlucky: a shell landed clear of its target, plummeting down well beyond the railyards. It landed in one of the narrow streets flanking the depot, exploding as it hit the ground. It was fired from a two-pounder howitzer, the case primed with fragmentary load. It went off directly in front of *Coronel* Alcaza, lifting him ten feet backwards with pieces of metal and shards of ruptured stone driving through his body. He was picked up and blown against a tumbling wall so that the spraying blood got lost inside the destruction of the building as it came down to cover his corpse with a mess of blood-stained rubble.

Onslow looked at Juan Oveda.

The man was grinning like a lunatic, plucking at his beard and crouching down as the shells landed, his body shaking as though each explosion might bring fresh suffering.

It didn't seem worth the journey.

Didn't seem worth the chances.

Not the risks or the gambles.

But he had made a promise. And he kept his word.

When he could.

'Let's go,' he said. 'Let's go take him to Villa.'

They got Oveda up on a horse, lashing him to the saddle because he didn't seem in full control of his body, then rode out to the east, cutting through the outskirts of the city.

León was in total confusion now. The Villista guns were laying down a solid bombardment, concentrated mainly on the storage sheds around the rail depot and the centre of the town. The defenders were answering with a barrage of their own, so that the evening sky was lit bright with the constant flash of cannon fire, the air heavy with the reek of cordite and burning, deafening with the sullen crump of exploding shells.

Onslow followed the trail back to the ridge and called a halt.

'We'll wait until morning,' he said. 'No point to chancing some trigger-happy *dorado* shooting us in the dark.'

They made camp, no one speaking much, but all casting surreptitious glances at Oveda. The Mexican squatted by the fire, picking at his beard and chuckling each time a fresh blast of artillery fire lit the ridge. He was clearly halfway mad, perhaps gone all the way down the dark avenues of insanity. Jamie handed him a mug of coffee that he took like a child accepting a new toy, handling the tin cup and sniffing at the hot liquid before cautiously tasting it. And then – like a child, still – he smiled and said, '*Gracias, jefe.*'

'You think it was worth it?' Strong stretched on the grass beside Onslow. 'To bring him out?'

'I don't know,' replied the lean-faced man. 'We got payed to do a job. That's all I know.'

'An' we did it,' murmured Strong. 'Like always.'

'Like always,' nodded Onslow. 'But hell, Jonas, I'm getting too old and too tired for this.'

Strong shrugged, grinning. 'We deliver, Cade. You'll feel different in the morning.'

'Maybe. I hope so.' Onslow sipped coffee, watching the battle below him. 'But right now I feel like I've seen one too many mornings.'

'Ain't we all?' murmured Strong.

And the night was quiet again, except for the steady thunder of the guns.